He was getting turned on watching her

In fact, Guy had been turned on since the moment Cassie had shown up at his door. He shifted in his seat, hoping she wouldn't notice how aroused he was becoming, and tried to focus on their conversation.

"You deserve better than that, Cassie."

Her eyes met his, questioning. Challenging. "Do I?"

Suddenly he knew words weren't the answer she wanted. It was time for action.

Their lips met and he heard her sigh. Or maybe that was him.

She pressed against him eagerly, her lips soft as velvet, warm and pliant beneath his own. He opened his mouth and she followed his lead. Their tongues met, hesitant at first, then with more eagerness. He hadn't been wrong. Cassie was a woman of passion. He'd been out of his mind to think he could resist a temptation like this.

"Guy?" Her voice was breathy as she broke off their kiss. Her tongue darted out to lick at her lips, a gesture that sent another jolt of desire through him. "Why don't we go into the bedroom?"

Dear Reader,

I've always admired people who had the courage to go after their dreams. Moving away from the comfort of routine and taking risks to make a dream come true demands a special kind of bravery.

Writing has always been my dream, so I'm especially pleased that my first Temptation novel deals with two people going after their own goals and desires. Writing this book also gave me a chance to set a story in one of my favorite places, Colorado, and to write about one of my favorite pastimes, downhill skiing.

I fell in love with Guy and Cassie as they pursed each other and their dreams. I hope you'll love them, too. I'd enjoy hearing from you. Write to me care of Harlequin Books, 225 Duncan Mill Road, Don Mills, Ontario, M3B 3K9, Canada, or e-mail me at CindiMyers1@aol.com. And visit me on the Web at www.TemptationAuthors.com.

Happy reading,

Cindi Myers

It's a Guy Thing!
Cindi Myers

HARLEQUIN®

F
MYB

TORONTO • NEW YORK • LONDON
AMSTERDAM • PARIS • SYDNEY • HAMBURG
STOCKHOLM • ATHENS • TOKYO • MILAN • MADRID
PRAGUE • WARSAW • BUDAPEST • AUCKLAND

For Amy, Debby, Carole, Gail, Patty, Lynda and Terri.
Thanks for being my cheerleaders.

ISBN 0-373-69102-5

IT'S A GUY THING!

Copyright © 2002 by Cynthia Myers.

This edition published by arrangement with Harlequin Books S.A.

® and TM are trademarks of the publisher. Trademarks indicated with
® are registered in the United States Patent and Trademark Office, the
Canadian Trade Marks Office and in other countries.

Visit us at www.eHarlequin.com

Printed in U.S.A.

1

THE SLEIGH BELLS attached to the door of the Java Jive jangled wildly as Cassie Carmichael burst into the coffee shop. She shoved through the swinging half door marked Employees Only, tossed her coat and purse aside, jerked her apron from the hook on the wall and slammed her empty coffee mug down on the counter. Her T-shirt read Women For Disarmament but the look on her face said she was in the mood to shoot first and ask questions later.

"Forget to take your happy pill this morning?" Her best friend and co-worker, Jill Sheldon, filled Cassie's mug with espresso and added steamed milk and a generous dollop of chocolate syrup.

Cassie glared at her friend and grabbed the cup with both hands. She took a long drink, then set it down with a *thunk*, sending the mocha sloshing onto the marble counter. "Do you think I'm too ordinary?" she demanded.

Jill turned from the coffee grinder, one perfectly arched brow raised in question. "Too ordinary? What do you mean?"

"Just what I said. Am I too ordinary?" Cassie held her arms down by her sides, palms out, inviting inspection. "Is there anything at all about me that would make the average person take a second look, or am I the kind of person other people naturally take for granted?"

"Hmm." Jill poured water into the coffee machine and flipped the switch to start a fresh pot. "Let me guess. Boring Bob is taking you for granted."

"I wish you wouldn't call him that. He's not boring." Cassie grabbed a cloth and began mopping up her spill.

"He is and you know it. What's he done this time?"

It wasn't so much what Bob had done, it was more what he hadn't done. Though Cassie had been dating him for more than two years now, he *hadn't* done anything to indicate that his feelings for her were serious. Lately, he treated her more like a personal assistant than a girlfriend.

"What did Bob do?" Jill prompted.

"He asked me to pick up his dry cleaning on my way home yesterday."

Jill nodded. "And of course, you did it."

"Yeah, I did it." She took another sip of coffee, then moved over to straighten a stack of napkins, avoiding Jill's gaze. "It's not that I really even minded doing it, it's just..." The hurt formed a lump in her throat she could hardly talk around. All those times she'd swallowed her pride and never complained had rushed back today, threatening to overwhelm her.

Jill moved over and put a hand on her shoulder. "Just what? He forgot to say thank you? He complained because the cleaners put too much starch in his shirts?"

She took a deep breath. "When I got to his apartment

with the cleaning, he was watching a movie with his friend Don. I laid the cleaning on the back of the couch and Bob said, 'Good old Cassie. She always takes care of me.'"

Jill winced. "Doesn't Bob already have a mother? Now he needs you to be another one?"

"That's not the worst of it." Cassie leaned back against the counter, arms folded under her breasts. "On my way into the kitchen, Don called out, 'Good old Cassie, bring me a beer, why don't you?' And I brought it to him!" She curled her hands into fists, heart pounding at the memory. "I should have poured it over his head."

"Yes, you should have." Jill patted her shoulder and moved over to tend the coffee machine. "Next time, you will."

If there was a next time. "What am I going to do?" Cassie asked. "Lately, when I'm with Bob, I feel like...like I'm invisible or something."

"Even when you're in bed?"

Cassie felt her face heat. "There hasn't been much, um, activity in that department lately."

Jill's eyebrows rose. "No wonder you're so grouchy."

Before Cassie could think of a retort, two women came in and Jill left to take their order. Cassie retrieved a tray of bagels from the cooler and began to fill the glass jar on the counter. It wasn't as if she and Bob never had sex...though it had been a while. When they first got together, the sex had been good. Pretty good anyway. Bob wasn't exactly creative, but he'd been energetic enough.

Now whenever she tried to get something going with him, he said he was too tired, or he ended up having to work late. At first, she'd taken his dedication to his job as a good sign. He was planning for the future—their future. Now, she was beginning to wonder if there was something wrong with her. Maybe Bob wasn't the only boring one in this relationship.

After the two customers left, Jill refilled her cup and perched on a stool behind the counter. "Have you thought of coming right out and asking Bob what's wrong? You know—talking about it?"

Cassie ducked her head and picked at a scuffed place on the edge of the counter. "I've thought of it. I just haven't gotten around to doing it yet."

"Are you afraid of what he'll say?"

She winced. "No...yes...I don't know." She slid onto the stool next to Jill. "What if this isn't Bob's fault? What if it's me?"

Jill frowned. "How do you figure that?"

She sighed and removed the glass dome from a plate of chocolate donuts. If she was going to hold her own little pity party, she might as well enjoy the appropriate refreshments. "Maybe if I'd finished college and gone on to a real career...." She pinched off a bite of donut and popped it into her mouth. "Maybe then Bob would think I'm more interesting and exciting."

Jill made a sour face. "Bob has a diploma and a so-called career and he's about as exciting as shower mold." She reached over and helped herself to half the donut. "And it's not as if you're a total slacker. You're going to school."

"I don't think Bob thinks massage therapy school is quite the same as college."

"When you graduate, you'll probably help more people than any accountant ever would. How's school going?"

Cassie shrugged. "It's going okay." But at one time or another, she'd said the same about secretarial school, medical technology school and the real estate licensing program she'd attended. She'd never stuck with any of them for very long.

In fact, she'd stayed with Bob longer than any attempt at a career. It had seemed easier somehow to hang on to a sure thing than to risk being alone again. But would being alone be so much worse than being ignored?

"If you really want to fix things between you two, it sounds like you need to do something to heat things up a little," Jill said.

Cassie replaced the dome on the donut plate. "Yeah, but what can I do?"

Jill traced a finger around the rim of her cup. "How about a little seduction? Remind him of what he's been missing."

"What—?" The word was cut off by the door bells again. Couldn't people go somewhere else to get their coffee this morning?

Her annoyance vanished, however, when she recognized this particular customer. Guy Walters turned feminine heads wherever he went, and in the years she'd known him her reaction had progressed from heart fluttering to an all-out cardiac drum solo. Maybe it was the way his dark brown hair fell across his forehead. Or the way his laser-blue eyes looked at people, as if they really mattered. Maybe it was his broad-shouldered, narrow-hipped body, honed to masculine perfection by hiking, biking, climbing, skiing and every other outdoor activity yet invented. Or maybe it was that when Guy spoke, Cassie felt as warm and wonderful as if she'd just downed a cup of Godiva hot chocolate with extra cream.

"Good morning, Guy." She slid off her stool and hurried to take his order. Not that she needed to ask what he wanted. Every Tuesday and Thursday he came in for a breve mocha and a sausage roll on his way to work at Mountain Outfitters, the business he had founded and made into a regional success. She knew he wore CK One cologne, that the scar underneath his chin was from a rock-climbing accident when he was in high school and that half the women in Boulder had been in love with him at one time or another.

"Hi, Cassie." He plucked a sausage roll from the glass jar on the counter. "Grande breve mocha." Cassie waited for his smile, which always left her a little breathless, but this morning the smile never came. What looked like an invitation on cream-colored paper with black engraving claimed his attention.

"Somebody graduating or getting married?" she asked as she prepared his coffee.

"What?" He looked up from studying the expensive-looking card. "Oh, it's a wedding invitation. From an old friend."

Judging by the mournful expression on Guy's face, she would have guessed it was a summons to a funeral. He tucked the invitation into the pocket of his leather jacket and picked up a flyer on the counter and began reading it. *So much for a memorable conversation,* Cassie thought. *I might as well be invisible. Let's face it. I'm ordinary, and Guy Walters is not.*

At Boulder High School, Guy had been part of a group of six upperclassmen who'd called themselves the Boulder Bandidos. They were behind every outrageous prank, from filling the science supply closet with two thousand Ping-Pong balls to attaching a pair of moose antlers to the front of Principle Harrington's Volvo. They were the first to take any dare, the first to try any new thing, from snowboarding to ice climbing.

Cassie had been three years younger, in the same class as Guy's sister Amy. She'd admired him from afar, following his exploits in the school paper and later, when he'd gone to the University of Colorado, keeping up with him through Amy or other friends.

She slid the cup of coffee across the counter and he paid, adding his change to her tip jar. "Thanks," she said, though she doubted he heard her. Head bent, he pushed open the door, bells chiming in his wake.

Jill came to stand behind her. "Why don't you ditch Boring Bob and go after a man like Guy?"

"As if he'd have anything to do with me." She picked up the carton of half-and-half and carried it to the refrigerator.

"Why not? You two have known each other a long time."

"I used to be friends with his sister. Years ago. Even back then, he hardly noticed me. And you saw how much attention he paid to me just now."

"You shouldn't sell yourself short," Jill said. "I'll bet

Guy would pay a lot of the right kind of attention if you gave him a little encouragement."

She sighed. Guy was her fantasy man. An impossible dream. She had to deal with real life, and for now, that meant Bob. She'd invested the past two years of her life in Bob. He was the man her mother thought she should marry. After all, he was good-looking and financially secure. So why hadn't that been enough for her lately? "How do you think I can get things back on track with me and Bob?"

Jill shrugged. "Show him what he's been missing by neglecting you. Seduce him."

"Seduce him?" Saying the word sent a shiver up her spine. It sounded so wild...so daring. "How?"

"I don't know." Jill waved her hand. "The usual. Sexy lingerie. Champagne. Why don't the two of you go away for the weekend? Some place romantic."

Cassie sagged against the counter and shook her head. "Can't. Bob's going up to Aspen Creek to work this weekend."

Jill made a face. "What kind of work is an accountant going to do at a ski resort?"

"He's rented a condo up there for the weekend. Said it was the only way he could catch up on all his paperwork." Cassie opened the dishwasher and began unloading coffee mugs. "He's been working really hard lately. I think he's bucking for a promotion."

"All work and no play are going to make that dull boy even duller." Jill began stacking the clean mugs on the shelves above the espresso machine. "Why don't you surprise him? Go up to the condo and convince him to take a break from the paperwork and work on what's left of your relationship."

"Maybe..." The idea sounded good, but was she brave enough to follow through with it? Could she seduce a man? Was this what she and Bob needed to set things right between them?

Even if the weekend was a bust, at least she'd know she'd tried. One way or another, she was bound to be better off come Monday. "All right. I'll do it." A shiver of excitement ran through her. Time to prove to Bob, and to herself, that she wasn't boring, that she *could* do something she set her mind to do. If she didn't, she might as well resign herself to spending the rest of her life as the invisible woman.

2

CASSIE WAS FAIRLY CERTAIN she wasn't crazy. Desperate, maybe, but not insane. "Tell me again that this is a good idea," she said as she and Jill pulled into the parking lot at Aspen Creek Resort two days later.

"Most men would be delighted if the woman they loved surprised them with a planned seduction," Jill said. "Although, I wouldn't say Bob is like most men. In fact, I'm a little surprised you're doing this."

Cassie stared at her. "But you're the one who suggested it."

Jill frowned. "Well, yeah. But I never thought you'd do it." She glanced up toward the lodge. "Are you sure Bob's worth it?"

"Of course he is," Cassie said, without much conviction. Bob had been acting so differently toward her lately, she couldn't be sure about anything. Except that she owed it to herself to try one last time to make things work between them. She opened the door and climbed out of the car.

"You know, you could find someone better." Jill looked at her over the top of the car. "Someone who would really appreciate your efforts."

"You mean, seduce a complete stranger?" Cassie

pulled on her gloves and zipped her jacket against the biting cold.

"No. But there are probably a lot of men who'd be interested in you if you'd give them a chance."

"Name one."

"Guy Walters."

Cassie laughed. "Guy Walters doesn't know I'm alive."

"Don't be so sure about that. I've seen him watching you."

A shiver danced through her at the thought. "You lie."

"Trust me. I know a lot about men and I think Guy's really interested in you. And he'd be a lot better for you than Bob."

Sure. As if Guy Walters didn't already have half the women in town after him. An ordinary woman didn't have a chance. She shrugged. "Bob's who I'm stuck with now, so I'm going to make the best of it." Even to her own ears, she didn't sound enthusiastic.

"Are you sure you don't want me to wait around, in case things don't work out?" Jill followed her around to the trunk. Fresh snow crunched under their boots and a gust of wind blew more snow down onto them from the trees.

"You don't have to wait. I'll be fine." Besides, if she knew Jill was still here, she might chicken out before she ever got to Bob's room. She hefted her backpack out of the trunk and checked its contents: bottled water, energy bars, champagne, strawberries, scented candles, some extra clothes and a change of underwear.

"What have you got in there?" Jill tried to peer over her shoulder, but Cassie quickly zipped up the pack.

"Don't forget these, Miss Girl Scout." Jill reached into the trunk and tossed her the box of condoms that must have slipped from the pack.

Cassie blushed and shoved the box into the pack's outside pocket. "Bob always forgets," she mumbled.

"He doesn't forget. He just knows he doesn't have to be prepared because you always are." Jill stepped back as Cassie closed the trunk. "I don't know why you're going to so much trouble for him."

She shouldered the pack and adjusted the straps. "You said it yourself. I can't let things go on the way they have been. After this weekend, Bob won't take me for granted anymore."

Jill squinted up at the gray sky. "It looks like it might storm. I don't like the idea of leaving you up here all alone."

"I won't be alone. Bob's here. Somewhere." She turned to study the log chalet at the base of the ski slopes. Good thing Aspen Creek was a small resort, with only this one building of condos. She'd never have found Bob at some big place like Vail or Copper Mountain.

"I still say what kind of guy goes to a ski resort to spend the weekend working?"

Cassie hugged her arms around herself and stamped her feet as a blast of icy wind gusted across the road. "Bob's been really wrapped up in his job lately. This weekend will be a good chance for us to talk about our relationship."

"From the looks of that pack, you don't intend to spend much time talking."

Cassie's cheeks burned. So maybe talk wasn't all she had in mind. Was there anything wrong with a woman surprising her longtime boyfriend with a little seduction? Somebody had to do something before whatever they'd once had between them died of neglect. "This was your idea, remember? And I thought it would be good to try something different."

"This is different, all right. It's not like you at all."

Cassie knew what that meant. It wasn't like quiet, dependable, conventional Cassie to take off for a wild weekend fling. "Maybe this *is* like me," she said. "The real me."

Jill didn't look any less worried. "Just be careful." She gave Cassie a quick hug. "Call me if you need anything."

Cassie nodded. "I will. And thanks."

"Call me Monday, anyway." Jill opened the driver's-side car door. "I want a full report."

Cassie laughed and started up the road toward the lodge. At the top of the hill, she turned to wave at Jill, then took a deep breath and headed off for what was going to be either the greatest thrill of her life, or the biggest embarrassment.

Skiers crowded into the lodge office, some fresh from the slopes, clomping across the carpet in snow-dusted ski boots, others gathered around a massive stone fireplace, enjoying hot toddies or cold beers. A picture window behind the registration desk showed fresh snow falling on the groomed slopes, a line of skiers at the lift waiting for another run down the mountain.

Cassie stood in line at the front desk behind an older couple in matching sweatshirts that bore the legend, We're Spending Our Children's Inheritance. Would she and Bob ever be like that, so close after years together that they were practically twins? She frowned. Somehow, she couldn't picture it.

She shifted, trying to surreptitiously adjust the teddy she wore beneath her sweater and leggings. The black silk lingerie, cut up to here and down to there was a far cry from her usual plain-Jane underwear. She felt supersexy wearing it.

"Are you telling me there's not one single room available in the entire resort?" The voice of the older man in front of her rose over the murmur of conversation in the lobby.

"I'm sorry, Mr. Kates, but we're booked solid. We don't have any rooms available until next Wednesday."

"Come along, dear. I'm sure we can find a room in Winter Park." The woman tugged at her husband's arm. "Next time we'll call ahead."

"I guess we'd better," the husband grumbled, turning away from the desk. "I want to get settled for the night before that storm blows in."

"Yes, Miss, can I help you?"

Cassie stepped up to the desk. "I believe Bob Hamilton is registered here?" She put on her best "trust me, I'm an honest person" smile and proceeded to lie. "He's expecting me."

The clerk punched the keys of a computer. "Oh, yes,

Ms. Patterson. He mentioned you would be arriving today."

The smile remained frozen on Cassie's face, mainly because she was too stunned to move. "Ms. P-Patterson?"

"Yes." The clerk looked up from the computer. "You are Mary Ann Patterson, aren't you?"

"Yes. Of course." What was another lie when she was in this so deep already?

"Suite 418." The clerk handed her a key and slid a computer printout toward her. "If you'll sign here."

She scrawled something she hoped was unintelligible and picked up the key. Maybe there'd been some mistake. Maybe they'd gotten the name wrong. Maybe there were *two* Bob Hamiltons here this weekend.

Right. And maybe she'd win the lottery next week and wake up four inches taller and five pounds lighter.

She took the stairs up to the fourth floor two at a time, heart pounding from more than exertion. If she was going to chicken out, now was the time to do it. She could find a phone, call Jill to come pick her up and Bob would never know.

Nothing would be any different between them and she'd either go on being "good old Cassie" or she'd go berserk one day and strangle him with his own dry cleaning.

No. She straightened and settled the pack more firmly on her shoulders. She wasn't going to quit this time.

Suite 418 was at the end of a carpeted hallway. She slowed her steps, trying to remember what she'd planned to say, but all she could come up with was *who the hell is Mary Ann Patterson?*

A petite brunette emerged from the elevator in front of her. She wore high-heeled black leather boots and brown suede leggings that clung to her thighs like a second skin. Her fisherman's sweater looked expensive and her perfectly styled hair could only have come from a high-class salon. She was the kind of woman who had never in her life been in danger of being invisible.

Cassie hung back, wanting this stranger to be safely in her room before she confronted Bob. The woman strode down the hall, a tapestry flight bag wheeling behind her. The farther down the hall she walked, the tighter the knot in Cassie's stomach grew. By the time the woman knocked on the door of 418, Cassie wasn't even surprised.

"Sweetie, so glad you made it ahead of the storm!" Bob's voice echoed down the hallway as the door opened. Cassie ducked behind a potted palm, peeking through the fronds to watch Bob envelop Puss in Boots in a hug. She didn't even bother trying to convince herself that the woman might, after all, be a business associate, since one of Bob's hands was firmly caressing the woman's suede-clad behind.

She wasn't sure if the lump in her throat was a stifled scream or incipient nausea. Rather than let loose with either in the hallway, she bolted back along the corridor and down the stairs. What a mess she was in now—stranded with a snowstorm on its way, a bottle of champagne rapidly warming in her backpack, a French lace teddy creeping up her butt and no room at the inn.

GUY WALTERS unlocked the door to the family condo and dumped his bags in the entryway. He'd spent so many weekends here over the years that the rooms were as familiar to him as his own apartment. His dad had taught him to ski here at Aspen Creek. His mother had taken him ice skating on the resort's pond. A weekend here always meant sleigh rides, marshmallow roasts and hot chocolate. Even after he'd moved out on his own, this was a place where he could always find happy memories and a warm welcome.

Today, the condo was cold and the air smelled of dust and disinfectant. The furniture looked old and worn. The rooms were too empty, reminding him that he was past the age when he'd expected to be coming to Aspen Creek with a wife and children of his own in tow.

He frowned and went to turn up the thermostat. Back in Boulder, getting away for the weekend had seemed like a good idea. He'd planned to ski a little, catch up on his reading, grab a few drinks in the bar and kick back and relax. Now that he was here, though, with the snow coming down and long days in this empty apartment stretching out ahead of him, the idea felt like a recipe for depression.

He shrugged off his jacket and started to toss it onto the sofa, but the crackle of paper distracted him. He removed the envelope from the pocket and tapped it against his palm. So Dave was getting married. The last of the Boulder Bandidos, besides Guy himself, to take the plunge. Steve and Victor were already fathers and last he'd heard, Jake's wife was expecting. They'd traded nights on the town for Happy Meals and evenings around the VCR, watching *The Lion King* video for the twenty-seventh time.

He sank down onto the sofa, still staring at the envelope. The scary thing was, that kind of cozy evening at home was starting to sound not so bad to him. Better than a weekend at a snowed-in resort, with no one to share it with.

He tossed the invitation onto the coffee table and shoved his hands into his pockets. If he was going to spend the weekend moping, he'd be better off heading back to Boulder now. He had plenty of work to occupy him at the store and in town he could probably find a couple of pals to hang out with tomorrow night.

He walked to the window and pulled back the long drapes. The snow was coming down so hard he could barely make out the ski slopes beyond. They'd already shut down the lift, not a good sign. Chances of getting home in this whiteout seemed pretty slim.

He fetched the sack of groceries from the entryway and began unloading the contents into the refrigerator. While he worked, he popped open a beer and took a long drink. Maybe being stranded here alone this weekend wouldn't be so bad. It would give him a chance to take a good look at his life and where he was headed.

He closed the fridge and sagged back against the door, frowning. The problem was, he didn't have to look at his life very closely to know he didn't particularly like what he saw.

CASSIE SANK INTO an empty chair by the lobby fireplace and tried to think what to do next. She could call Jill, but her friend hadn't even had a chance to make it home yet. Besides, from the looks of the snow falling outside, the roads wouldn't stay open much longer. She was stuck here for the night. While she was trying to sleep in this uncomfortable chair, Bob and "Sweetie" would be warming the sheets upstairs. The thought made her want to gag.

She stared into the fire, as if she might find Bob's face smoldering among the flames. She'd told herself coming up here that this weekend was her last chance to save their relationship, and it turned out there was nothing left to save.

Looking back, she could see the signs—his sudden interest in work, his unexplained absences and most of all, the fact that their sex life had been all but nonexistent for the past six months. She'd known something was wrong, but she'd refused to admit it. She didn't want to make waves. Didn't want a scene.

She gulped down the knot in her throat. Those days were over. No more meek little mouse. She was going to make one hell of a scene when she saw him again.

"Say, Jack, you got any matches? I went to light a fire and couldn't find any anywhere."

That deep, velvety voice sent a tremor through Cassie's middle. At first, she thought despair had driven her to some kind of auditory hallucination. After all, what would Guy Walters be doing up here? But when she turned to look around the side of the chair, her fantasy man was standing at the front desk, accepting a folder of matches from the clerk.

"Thanks," Guy said. "Want to get a beer or something after you get off work?"

The clerk grinned. "Thanks, Guy, but I can't. My fiancée's cooking dinner for me."

"Fiancée? When did this happen?"

The clerk's grin broadened. "About a month ago. The wedding's set for June."

"Congratulations."

"Thanks, Guy. You'll have to meet Cheryl. She's a great gal."

"I'll bet she is. Well, thanks for the matches." He turned and walked away from the desk. Cassie leaned over farther, watching him disappear down the hall. So Guy Walters was here. Was he alone? He hadn't mentioned anyone else when he'd asked the clerk to have a beer with him. Maybe it was wishful thinking on her part, but she'd have sworn Guy sounded...lonely.

She grabbed up her backpack and followed Guy down the hall and up the stairs. She told herself she only wanted to see where he was staying, but already the kernel of an idea was growing in her mind. *Why not go after a man like Guy?* Jill had said.

He emerged from the stairwell on the fourth floor. She followed and watched him disappear into a room at the opposite end of the hall from Bob's. She glanced over her shoulder, toward suite 418. *What were Bob and "Sweetie" up to now?* she wondered. As if she couldn't guess.

As she stared at the brass-plated numbers on the door, a new surge of anger filled her. She had half a mind to knock on that door and tell her so-called boyfriend exactly what she thought of him and his two-timing ways. She clenched her hands into fists and took a step toward his door. He thought he was so clever, pulling this scam on dumb old Cassie, but she'd show him—

Just then, the door swung open. "I'm going to get some ice," Bob's voice drifted to her. Clad in boxer shorts and a T-shirt, he stepped into the hall, ice bucket in hand.

Cassie made a strangled noise as Bob turned toward her. "Cassie!" he gasped. "What are you doing here?"

Her first instinct was to turn and run, but some semblance of self-respect asserted itself and she stood her ground. "I came here to tell you what a worthless creep you are." She drew in a shaky breath. "And that I never want to see you again."

She turned away, but he lunged forward and caught her arm. "Aw, Cassie, what are you talking about?" He gave her an everything's-going-to-be-all-right smile and patted her shoulder—as if she were a four-year-old, or a particularly troublesome puppy. "Why don't we go somewhere and talk about what's gotten you so upset?"

She looked down, wondering if it would be worth the effort to knee him where it would hurt the most. Her eyes narrowed. "Since when do you wear black silk boxers?" She glared at him. "You never wore silk boxers for *me*."

"Now, hon, did you ever ask me?" He tried to put his arm around her, but she jerked away.

"Don't touch me!"

"There's no need to shout." He frowned and glanced over his shoulder. "Someone might hear."

"Oh, I don't mind." She cupped her hands to her mouth and shouted. "Come on out, Mary Ann, and watch your new boyfriend act like the two-timing jerk he is!"

Bob's smile collapsed at the mention of his partner in crime. "Now, Cassie!" He made shushing motions toward her. "I really think you're being unreasonable."

"Unreasonable." She took a deep breath, rage making her feel two inches taller and ten times stronger. "I'll tell you what's unreasonable. Unreasonable is me waiting on you hand and foot for two years and expecting to get anything out of it. Unreasonable is me trying to be the woman *you* wanted instead of the woman I am."

"Why don't you go on back home and we'll talk about it next week?" A feeble imitation of a smile returned to his lips. "I'll take you to dinner. How about that?"

"You're an idiot, Bob. Goodbye." Damn, it felt good to say that! And it felt even better to see the horror on his face when he realized she was serious. She gave him her own patronizing smile and started to turn away, when his door opened again.

"Who are you talking to?" The brunette she'd seen earlier peered out of the room, one naked shoulder showing in the doorway. "I thought I heard shouting."

"Uh, no one, darling." Bob rushed to the door and began pushing Mary Ann back inside. "Just some crazy woman."

"That's right, some crazy woman." Cassie broadened her smile and fluttered her fingers at the other woman. "A crazy woman who's finally regained her sanity."

With one last fearful look in her direction, Bob succeeded in forcing Mary Ann back into the room and shut the door firmly behind them. Cassie began to laugh, happiness bubbling up inside her like champagne. God, that felt good! And to think she'd wasted all these years keeping her mouth shut when things didn't turn out the way she wanted.

She turned and walked down the hall again, intending to head downstairs, but instead found herself drawn to the opposite end of the hall, to the condo where Guy Walters was staying. Guy Walters, her dream man. Here alone for the weekend. And so was she.

She stopped in front of the door to Guy's suite. Why *not* go after Guy? After all, hadn't she said she wasn't going to hold back anymore? Given the choice between spending the night in a chair in the lobby, and spending the night with the man of her dreams, what woman wouldn't pick Guy?

Here was an opportunity to turn all her fantasies into reality. If she passed up this chance, she might as well put her hair up in a bun, let the hems down on all her skirts and resign herself to going through the rest of her life in a painfully proper stupor.

Before reason could overwhelm desire, she stepped forward and knocked on Guy's door. As soon as her knuckles came in contact with the wood, a shiver of panic swept over her. She would have turned and fled, but her feet refused to listen to her brain and move. The door swung open and Guy stared down at her. "Hello?" he said.

She opened her mouth, but no sound came out. Her heart was beating somewhere in the vicinity of her throat, and all she could do was gape.

3

GUY LEANED TOWARD HER, his brow furrowed. "Cassie? Are you all right?"

"Um...I...uh..." Suddenly, she couldn't think of a single coherent sentence. She stared up at him, into those warm brown eyes. He didn't look angry or annoyed, just...concerned. As if...as if he might really care what she wanted. "Can I come in?" she blurted.

He opened the door wider. "Yeah. Sure."

She slipped past him and went to stand in front of the fire that was beginning to blaze in the fireplace.

Guy shut the door and walked over to her. "You look upset. Are you in some kind of trouble?" He glanced over his shoulder. "I thought I heard shouting in the hall just now. Was that you?"

She hugged her arms across her stomach and stared at the floor, fighting sudden tears. "No, I'm not in trouble. At least not yet. And yes, that was me shouting."

He looked at her warily. "Want to tell me what's going on?"

She sighed. Maybe it would help to talk about it. That's all. Just talk. "I was shouting at my boyfriend. *Ex*-boyfriend. Bob Hamilton. He said he was coming up here this weekend to work, so I thought I'd follow him up here and surprise him." She frowned. "Instead,

I'm the one who was surprised." She buried her face in her hands. "I can't believe I was so stupid I didn't realize he was seeing someone else."

She peeked through her fingers at him, steeling herself for a look of pity. Instead, he looked sympathetic and...*interested?* "You never struck me as stupid," he said.

She lowered her hands. "I didn't? I mean...I never thought you noticed."

His smile could have melted icicles. "I noticed."

The words set her heart to pounding and she had trouble catching her breath. *Please don't anybody pinch me,* she thought. Any minute now, she'd wake up and this dream would be over. She slowly slid her hands from her face and risked looking at Guy full-on. He was still smiling at her, a heart-melting look that sent rational thought ducking for cover before a full-fledged assault of giddy fantasy and old-fashioned lust. Oh, God, what had she gotten herself into?

The new Cassie might be ready for this, but the parts of old Cassie that still hung around belonged to a coward. "Uh, I didn't mean to barge in on you like this. I'll go now and get out of your way." She lunged toward the door.

Guy's hand on her arm stopped her. "You don't have to go. To tell you the truth, I was feeling kind of lonely before you showed up."

So she'd been right. He *was* lonely. But how was that possible? The man had dozens of friends, hundreds even. He could have any woman he wanted. Maybe he was only being nice....

She squared her shoulders and mentally shook herself. What did it matter why he'd invited her to stay? He'd invited her. It's what she'd wanted all along, wasn't it?

She forced herself to meet his gaze and faked a confident smile. "I'd love to stay."

He came closer. She would have moved back, but already the fire was in danger of singeing her legs. He reached for her and for one heart-stopping moment, she thought he might gather her into his arms and kiss her, as he had so many times in her fevered fantasies.

Instead, he took hold of the straps of her backpack. "Why don't you take this off?"

She let him help her out of the pack while she tried to find her voice. The realization that she was here—alone—with the man of her dreams made it hard to breathe, much less talk. She grabbed hold of the fireplace mantel to steady herself.

"Can I get you something to drink?" he asked.

Drink. Right. Maybe a drink would help. "There's some champagne in my bag." No reason to let it go to waste.

She bent and fumbled for the backpack, but he was quicker. Unzipping the bag, he pulled out a pair of white silk panties and the bottle of champagne. "Nice," he murmured.

Was he talking about the underwear or the wine? She grabbed the panties from him and stuffed them back into the pack. "Sorry."

He grinned. "I'll go get some glasses." As he headed for the kitchen, she could have sworn he was whistling.

GUY SMILED TO HIMSELF as he hunted in the cupboard for glasses. Of all the crazy things to happen. Just when he'd been ready to give up on the weekend, cute little Cassie Carmichael showed up. Except she wasn't so little anymore, a fact he'd noticed a while back at the coffee shop.

When he'd first walked into Java Jive a few months ago, he hadn't even connected the curvy clerk behind the counter with his kid sister's school friend. But as soon as she'd said his name and smiled, he'd remembered. What a difference a few years had made.

More than once since then, he'd thought of asking her out, but he wasn't sure how his sister would feel about it. Amy and Cassie apparently weren't friends anymore, so maybe there was bad blood there. Before he could find out, he'd heard Cassie was already involved with someone and he figured he'd missed his chance.

Now fate had literally delivered the lovely Ms. Carmichael to his door. He wasn't about to blow a second chance to get to know Cassie better. Amy would have to understand.

He shook his head as he rinsed glasses. Funny, he'd thought of Cassie as the quiet, shy type. Obviously, he'd been wrong, judging by the contents of her pack and her plans to surprise her lowlife boyfriend.

By the time he returned with two glasses filled with champagne, she'd settled into a chair by the fire, arms wrapped around her knees. He handed her a glass of champagne and offered a toast. "Cheers."

"Thanks for being so cool about this," she said. "I was upset after seeing Bob with that woman and not thinking clearly, and there wasn't another room available and I didn't have anywhere to go—"

"It's okay." He settled onto the sofa, at the end nearest her. "It's all right with me if you stay here." It was more than all right, really. Suddenly his lonely weekend didn't look so lonely.

She glanced toward the window. Snow was coming down in great drifts. "I guess none of us will be going anywhere for a while." She sank back into the chair and stared at the bubbles in the champagne. "We're trapped here."

"Hey, don't make it sound so terrible." He leaned forward, elbows on his knees. "I know I'm not Bob, but I'm not such a bad fellow." If you asked him, Bob was a first-class creep to skip out on a woman like this one. The thought made his jaw tighten in anger. How often did you come across such sweetness and sensuality wrapped up in one neat little package? "I don't mind sharing the condo with you until the storm passes." Which, with any luck, wouldn't be for a couple of days.

She looked around the room, perhaps taking in how small it was. Intimate. "I feel like I'm intruding. I mean, you obviously came up here to be alone." She flushed. "Or maybe you're expecting someone."

He shook his head. "I'm not expecting anyone." He shrugged. "It was sort of a last-minute thing. I had some vacation coming and decided to take the weekend off. You know—read, think about things." Even before he'd gotten the invitation from Dave, he'd been restless. Like something was missing from his life. Or somebody...

She ran her finger around the rim of her glass and

looked glum. "I guess I've got a few things to think about now, too."

"You mean Bob."

She nodded. "I can't believe I was so blind. So trusting. Good old Cassie." She gripped the arms of the chair, white-knuckled, jaw clenched. "He must have been laughing behind my back the whole time."

She glanced at Guy. "Jill calls him 'Boring Bob' sometimes. Never one to get excited about anything. Always so predictable. Boy, did we have him wrong."

"We all make mistakes." It was one of those platitudes that don't really mean anything, but it was all he could think of at the moment. He wanted to take away her hurt, to see her smile again. She had such a sweet smile. There was a better coffee shop closer to his office, but Cassie's smile always drew him back to Java Jive.

"I wanted to surprise him this weekend," she said, green eyes snapping with rage. "I thought I'd shake him up, put a little life back in our relationship. Hah!"

Guy braced himself. Any minute now, the waterworks would start. He felt in his pocket for a handkerchief, just in case.

Cassie Carmichael didn't burst into tears. Instead, she shot up out of the chair and began to pace. "When I think of all I did for that man! Oh, he owes me. Big time."

Guy followed her with his eyes as she stalked back and forth in front of the fireplace. Cheeks flushed, hair tumbling about her shoulders, she was a woman overcome by passion, though not of the romantic kind. You didn't see that kind of emotion every day. Most people sleepwalked through life, not allowing themselves to feel much of anything, but not Cassie. Here was a woman who wasn't asleep.

He was getting turned on watching her, had in fact been turned on since the moment she'd showed up at his door. He could still recall the feel of those silky panties between his fingers. The thought unnerved him. She had been his kid sister's friend. And yet, Cassie was practically a stranger to him. He had no business lusting after her. He shifted in his seat, hoping she wouldn't notice how aroused he was becoming.

"Listen to me, going on like this." She stopped in front of him. "Not only do I intrude on your weekend, I start dumping all my personal problems on you."

"No, that's all right." He stood and reached for the champagne bottle. "Let me refill your glass. If you're hungry, I've got some cheese and stuff."

"Yeah, I guess I am a little hungry at that. There are some strawberries in my pack."

She started toward the pack, but he intercepted her. "I'll get them. After all, you're my guest."

She smiled, apparently seeing the humor in the remark. It was a strange situation, but now that she was here, he was glad of it. Humming to himself, he retrieved the cheese, summer sausage and crackers from the grocery bags, then went to get the strawberries from her pack.

He didn't find them right away. First, he took out two scented candles, a bottle of cinnamon-flavored massage oil and the pair of almost-sheer white panties. The silk slid through his fingers, sending his temperature soaring.

He glanced over his shoulder to see if she'd noticed, but she was curled up in the chair again, staring into the fire.

All right, she'd just had her heart broken. It wouldn't be exactly fair for him to hit on her now, would it? No matter how much he was tempted. Reluctantly, he returned the panties to the pack and dug out the strawberries. Better to keep things pleasant and platonic, get to know each other before they took things any further.

Still, it would take everything he had to keep his hands to himself this weekend. He'd have to find something safe for them to do. Something that would keep his mind off of sex.

CASSIE LOOKED OVER her shoulder to where Guy stood in the condo's kitchen alcove. He hummed to himself as he sliced cheese, moving with fluid grace. Dressed in faded jeans and a flannel shirt, he could have been a model in a Ralph Lauren ad—tousled hair, broad shoulders, flat stomach and the most perfect male rear end in existence.

She pinched herself. Yep, she was awake, all right, though Guy had starred in more than one erotic dream in the years since she'd first met him.

She turned back toward the fire, hoping he wouldn't see her infatuation written on her face. It was one thing to fantasize about a man from a distance, quite another to be face-to-face with that man at a small, secluded resort.

Her heart thudded and she had to set aside her empty glass for fear of dropping it from her suddenly shaking hands. It didn't matter how small this condo was or how alone they were. Men like Guy weren't interested in quiet women like her. Her fantasies would have to stay fantasies, and that was all there was to it.

"Looks like you need a refill." He returned with the champagne bottle and a plate of cheese, fruit and crackers. He refilled her glass and she thought he'd sit back down on the sofa. Instead, he settled on the floor at her feet. "Is the fire warm enough for you?" he asked.

She opened her mouth to answer, but no sound emerged. Warm was not the word for what she was feeling. The closer he got, the higher her temperature rose.

Unfortunately, the feeling obviously wasn't mutual. "It's still a little chilly in here," he said. "I'll put some more wood on the fire."

He stood and fetched a log from a washtub on the hearth for the fire, then sat back at her feet and offered the plate of food. She bit into a strawberry and sipped more champagne. The bubbly was making her lightheaded. Or was that Guy?

She pulled her gaze away from him, toward the table beside her and a picture resting there. Six young men, dressed for the slopes, posed with a variety of snowboards and skis, clowning for the camera. "The Boulder Bandidos," Guy said, looking over her shoulder. "Up to their usual mischief."

"I recognize you." She put her finger on a thinner, gawkier version of the man beside her. Even then, he'd been handsome, though still more boy than man. "And the others look familiar from school, but I'm not sure I remember all their names."

"That's Steve." He pointed to the tallest of the group. "He's married now, with two kids. He works for one of the big eight accounting firms. That's Jake next to him. His wife is expecting their first baby any day now. The dude making the peace sign is Victor. He has his own business, doing something with the Internet. He and his wife, Daria, live in Denver with their little girl. The short, stocky guy is Paul. He married a girl named Sheila who already had two kids and they run a restaurant in Colorado Springs. And that's Dave." He pointed to a blonde standing next to him. "He's getting married in a couple of months to a woman from Boulder."

"Was that the invitation you were looking at the other morning?"

He nodded. "That's the one."

"You didn't seem too happy about it."

"It showed that much, huh?"

She smiled into her champagne glass, but didn't answer. Most people wouldn't have seen it, but she'd noticed everything about Guy for years.

"The invitation caught me off guard. I'd figured Dave was a confirmed bachelor."

"Like you?" She held her breath, waiting for his answer.

He shook his head. "I'm not a confirmed anything. I just haven't found the right woman." He turned away, to stir up the fire.

The words sent a quiver through her stomach. Guy had been her fantasy man all these years, her unobtainable ideal. Did he have a fantasy woman in his mind?

And was she even a little bit like her? "Are you looking?"

She wanted to take the words back as soon as she spoke. But she wanted to know the answer more.

He didn't say anything right away, and when she mustered up the courage to look at him, she was startled to find him watching her. His gaze caught and held her, going past the surface to see deeper. Her face heated and she fought the urge to look away. What was Guy looking for in her? Did she dare hope he would find it?

"Let's say I'm open to possibilities." He drained his glass and set it aside. "When I find the right woman, I'd like to settle down, have a family. What about you? What do you want to do with your life?"

Ugh. The million-dollar question and she didn't even have a ten-dollar answer. She forced a laugh, as if this was all such a fun game, instead of a depressing dilemma. "I haven't decided yet. There are so many possibilities."

"I think Amy mentioned you quit school."

She ran her fingers up and down the stem of her champagne glass. Quit was such as ugly word. "When I changed my major I needed a bunch of new courses for a degree. It would have meant an extra year of college. I was running out of money, so I left and enrolled in secretarial school instead."

His puzzled frown told her he was trying to make the connection between secretarial school and Java Jive, so she rushed forward with the rest of her explanation. He might as well know the worst. "I quit that, too. Then I tried a few other things. The job at the coffee shop isn't great, I know, but it pays the bills while I'm in massage therapy school.''

"Now that's interesting work."

She leaned toward him, studying his face for any hint of condescension. Either Guy was a great actor, or he really was interested. "Uh, yeah. I think it's interesting," she said. At least she'd stuck with it longer than anything to date. "I was thinking of going into sports medicine. I'd like to do something to help people."

He smiled, his eyes still fixed on her. Why was he staring at her? She ran her tongue over her teeth, checking for strawberry seeds, and fought the urge to comb her fingers through her hair. Enough about her. She wanted to know about *him*. "So...I hear your store is a real success."

He nodded. "Yeah. I can't believe how fast it's taken off. I think I really found a niche and filled it."

She glanced at the photo of the Boulder Bandidos again. "It probably helped that you're such an outdoorsman yourself. You know the kinds of equipment hikers and climbers and fishermen want."

"Don't forget skiing." He leaned toward her again, close enough she could make out the shadow of his beard beneath the skin along his jaw. "I remember you were pretty hot stuff on skis when you and Amy were on the racing team at CU."

His praise, not to mention his choice of words, sent a rush of warmth through her. Guy Walters thought she was hot stuff.

"Do you still race?"

The question banished the warm fuzzy feeling like a bucket of cold water on a campfire. "No." She picked at a thread on her sweater. "I gave it up a couple of years ago."

"Too bad. You were really good. Why'd you quit?"

There was that word again. She looked away. Why had she given up something she'd loved so much? "I guess I got interested in other things." It sounded lame, but then, excuses usually were.

"I know Amy really misses it."

The words jerked her from the brink of her self-pity pool. Amy Walters had torn ligaments in both knees after a spectacular fall during a race shortly before Cassie left the team. "I'm sorry," she said softly, remembering how her friend had laughed with joy as she flew down the slopes. Cassie had always admired Amy's daring, and her sense of humor. She had a little green troll doll she pinned to her jumpsuit for good luck. She loved to play practical jokes of people, and had once filled an opponent's ski boots with shaving cream. "Is she able to ski at all anymore?"

"She probably could, but when the trainer told her she'd never race again, she hung up her skis for good. I guess it hurt too much to give up her dream."

At least Amy had a dream, Cassie thought. All she had were fleeting interests and her fantasies of Guy. She turned to look out the window facing the slopes. If someone had hung a sheet behind the glass, it wouldn't have looked much whiter than it did now. No one was going anywhere for a while, why should they? They had food and drink and a nice warm fire. It was the perfect romantic setting.

With the wrong man.

She popped the last strawberry into her mouth and bit down hard. As if Bob was the *right* man.

"This is good champagne." Guy tipped the last of it into her glass. "I'm glad we didn't let it go to waste."

He turned back to the fire and she risked looking at him again. Maybe the champagne wasn't the only thing that shouldn't go to waste this weekend.

He turned around and caught her staring at him. "Is something wrong?" he asked.

"No. Nothing's wrong." She suppressed a smile. In fact, everything was suddenly very right. For once in her life, she was going to follow through on a fantasy and make it reality. She was going to seduce Guy Walters, or die trying.

4

"I KNOW WHAT YOU NEED," Guy said.

You do? Cassie blinked. Had he somehow read her mind? Did he know she was thinking of making love to him in front of that fire? They didn't have a bearskin rug, but what the heck, a blanket would do.

"You need something to take your mind off things." He stood. "Why don't we play a game?"

"A game?" Her voice quavered. "What kind of game?" *Strip poker? Spin the bottle? Doctor?*

He went over to the cabinet in the corner and opened it. "How about Scrabble?"

Scrabble? She stared at him, stunned. She was going to spend the weekend with a Greek god and he wanted to play Scrabble?

He laid out the board on the coffee table between them and began turning over tiles. She sat back, arms crossed over her chest. Scrabble. What could be more tame? More conventional. He wouldn't have invited Sarah Michelle Gellar or Catherine Zeta-Jones or some other sex goddess to play Scrabble, would he? But good old Cassie Carmichael was obviously a Scrabble kind of gal. The more she thought about it, the madder she became.

He dealt seven tiles to each of them and studied his

own selection, handsome brow furrowed in thought. Had she been horribly wrong? Was sex god Guy Walters even duller than Boring Bob? She glanced at her tiles. *K, S, T, C, L, M, I.*

"You go first," Guy said.

My, wasn't he a gentleman? But she didn't want him to be a gentleman. And for once, she wasn't interested in being a lady. She idly rearranged the letters on her tray until a word formed. Ah, now here was something. Grinning, she laid the letters out on the board. *L...I...C...K...S.*

"*Licks?*" Guy looked up at her.

Making sure he got the idea, she ran her tongue over her lips. "That's twenty-two points."

SHE HAD THE MOST luscious mouth.... Guy quickly looked away and shifted in his seat, trying to get comfortable. How could someone who looked like an elementary school teacher—a very sexy elementary school teacher—be so seductive? If she kept this up, he'd have to go out in the snow to cool off.

He concentrated on the letter tiles in front of him. Selecting *B, O* and *I,* he arranged them over the *L* she'd played. "*Boil,*" he announced.

"It is a little warm in here, isn't it?" Before he could offer to open a window or tamp down the fire, she stripped off her sweater, revealing some black satin confection obviously designed more to enhance than hide. He had an unimpeded view of smooth, ivory shoulders and the tops of full breasts. His mouth went dry and he jerked his gaze away, but his eyes didn't want to obey and before he knew it he was looking at her again. He could clearly see her erect nipples pressed against the satiny material. He curled his fingers against his palm, fighting the urge to touch her.

"It's your turn," she said softly.

He looked down at the board. Without him even realizing it, she'd added a new word. *"Naked,"* he read. He swallowed, but his mouth was too dry for it to do much good. Anxious now to get this game over with as quickly as possible, he selected two letters and spelled the word *nip*.

Her eyes—they were a really pretty shade of green, he noticed—sparkled with laughter. She studied her letters again, head tilted so that her hair fell back from her neck, revealing a section of creamy flesh under her jaw. He'd like to kiss her there, to feel her pulse throbbing against his lips....

She leaned forward to place her letters on the board, her breasts straining against the satin lingerie. Did she know how wild that was making him? He glanced up and met her gaze, drawing him toward her....

"You look a little warm yourself," she murmured, and reached across the table to unfasten the top two buttons of his shirt. She moved slowly, her fingers brushing against his suddenly feverish skin. She was right. It was burning up in here.

Obviously, Scrabble had been a bad idea. If he had any hope of keeping his hands off her, he needed to do something that would get him away from her entirely.

"I'd better get some more wood for the fire." He jumped up and headed for the door.

"Wait! We're not finished with our game." Cassie rose up on her knees, as if to follow him.

"I just remembered, they lock the wood room at dark." He grabbed his coat from the closet and was out the door before she could talk him into staying.

What had he gotten himself into? He'd tried to do the right thing, helping out a friend who'd just been jilted by a jerk. The problem was, his own attraction to Cassie kept getting in the way of his honorable intentions. The last thing he wanted was for her to think he was the kind of man who'd take advantage of her distress.

At the bottom of the stairs he pushed through the door to the outside and headed for the woodpile at the edge of the trees. There were plenty of split logs in the wood room, which as far as he knew never closed, but he needed fresh air to clear his head and cool off his heated libido. One thing for certain—this was going to be a very long night.

Cassie stared after Guy's retreating figure. So much for her career as a femme fatale. Could she help it if Scrabble wasn't the most erotic game in history?

Sighing, she plucked her sweater from the chair and pulled it on. She didn't have much experience at seduction, but she could have sworn Guy was really turned on for a minute there. What had happened to turn him off?

She went into the bathroom and studied her face in the mirror. Between the snow and the champagne and her fury at Bob, her makeup and hair were a little worse for wear, but she didn't think she looked bad enough to drive a man out into the snow. No, something else had sent Guy running in the other direction.

She opened the medicine cabinet, hoping to find a bottle of aspirin. Champagne always gave her a head-ache. Why didn't she ever remember that before it was too late?

A half-full bottle of ibuprofen sat next to a bottle of prescription cough syrup on the middle shelf. She read the name on the cough syrup, *Amy Walters*.

Did Guy's sister have anything to do with his reluc-tance to take things any further with Cassie? Did he think making it with his kid sister's friend was bad form?

Or did the fact that Cassie and Amy weren't such good friends anymore put him off? She shook two ibu-profen into her hand and replaced the bottle in the cab-inet. Maybe it didn't have anything to do with Amy at all. Maybe Guy was simply a nice man who didn't want to get involved with a woman who so obviously wasn't his type.

Her reflection in the mirror wore a lopsided smile. It figured. The one time in her life she was ready to settle for no-commitment sex, she met a decent man who didn't want to take advantage.

WHEN GUY RETURNED with an armload of freshly split logs, he found Cassie curled up on the sofa, eyes closed. He eased the wood into the washtub, then crept over to her. She'd put her sweater back on, and taken off her boots, revealing black socks embroidered with little pink bows. A lock of hair had fallen across her cheek and he resisted the urge to smooth it back into place.

Now that she was asleep, he felt at ease to watch her,

to let his eyes linger on the soft curve of her cheek or the rounded shape of her hip. A few hours ago, he'd been working on a serious case of the blues, dreading a weekend by himself, half afraid he'd spend the rest of his life alone. Then this woman had knocked on his door and changed the way he thought about the weekend, maybe even the way he thought about the rest of his life.

He reached down and pulled an afghan over her. Cassie snuggled against the pillow. "Thanks," she murmured.

"I didn't mean to wake you," he said.

"That's all right." She yawned and rolled over onto her back to look up at him. "I was lying here thinking, and I must have drifted off."

He sat down on the edge of the sofa. "What were you thinking about?"

The fire crackled as a log settled, and outside the window the wind howled. Cassie closed her eyes and didn't say anything.

"I did a lot of thinking while I was chopping wood, too," he said. He rubbed his hands together, trying to keep from touching her.

Her eyes flew open. "Oh?"

"I was thinking about why I came up here this weekend."

"Why is that?" Her voice was soft, breathy, like a caress.

"I was trying to figure out my life. What I wanted." A thought popped into his head, like a neon sign glowing bright, that what he wanted was Cassie. He quickly pushed it aside. He hardly knew the woman. How could she be the answer to the restlessness that had plagued him?

She sat up and swung her feet to the floor. Her shoulder brushed his, but he didn't move away. "I guess I came up here for pretty much the same reason," she said.

Jealousy pricked at him, sharp and painful. He didn't like remembering that she'd come here to be with another man.

As if reading his thoughts, she turned her head to look at him. "This weekend wasn't really about Bob," she said. "I didn't want to admit it to myself, but I think I knew things were over between us." She smoothed the afghan across her lap. "I told myself I was coming here to try to salvage our relationship, but I think I really wanted to prove to myself that I could do something daring. Something different."

"You mean this isn't how you usually spend your spare time?"

He purposely made the words teasing.

She looked away from him, at the fire. "When you first saw me at the coffee shop, what did you think?"

He smiled, remembering. "I thought my kid sister's friend had certainly grown up." He watched her out of the corner of his eye as he spoke. "I wanted to ask you out."

She stared at him. "You didn't."

"Yeah, I did." He laced his fingers together, wanting to reach for her but afraid she'd pull away. "I didn't know what Amy would think of it and before I could ask her, I heard you were already involved with someone."

Sadness shadowed her eyes. "Do you think Amy wouldn't approve of you going out with me?"

He took her hand in his then, unable to stop himself any longer. "Do you?"

Cassie held herself still, not pulling away from him, but not moving toward him either. "We didn't exactly part on good terms."

He tried to remember when Amy and Cassie had ceased to be friends, but he couldn't pin it down to a specific date. Cassie had stopped coming around and Amy had never mentioned her again. "What happened?"

She shrugged. "She didn't approve of my quitting the team."

"Was this after her accident?"

She nodded. "She was still in a wheelchair, after her surgery, but she came to team meetings and watched films and helped coach everybody." She looked at him, eyes glistening. "It was so hard seeing her like that. I thought she'd understand when I told her I couldn't race anymore."

He squeezed her hand, fighting a knot in his own throat. He'd cried for his sister once, but it had been a long time ago. "But she didn't."

She hung her head. "No. She told me I was settling for being ordinary, when I could have been extraordinary."

He cupped her chin and turned her head until their eyes met. "I think you're pretty extraordinary."

"No, I'm not. I'm a quiet, ordinary, even timid person. I'm the kind of person other people take for granted." Her eyes darkened, her expression intense.

"But sometimes, I feel like there's so much more. Like there's this other side of me trying to get out—a person who's daring and exciting. A person no one would ever take for granted." She frowned. "Does that make any sense?"

"Yeah. Yeah, it makes a lot of sense." He squeezed her hand. "Maybe this other side of you just needs a little encouraging."

"I don't know how to do that." The sadness in her voice tore at him.

He pulled back and looked at her intently. "Was there ever anything you really wanted to do in your life, but you never did it?"

She looked puzzled. "What do you mean?"

He thought a moment, trying to find the right words. "Something like...well, even when I was in high school, I wanted to own my own business. Something to do with adventure and the outdoors. I was still in college when I started going around to banks, trying to get financing for a store that would offer all sorts of outdoor gear. Everyone said I was crazy—I was too young, I had no experience. But it was my dream, and I didn't let what others said stop me."

She nodded. "And now your store's a big success and everyone's saying you're a genius."

"Not everyone. But I'm proud I didn't let others talk me out of my dream." He cradled her hands between both his own, savoring the smoothness of her skin. "Now it's your turn. What's your dream that hasn't come true yet?"

She thought a moment, obviously reluctant. "Well...

I want to be a massage therapist. I mean, it's something I really think I'll stick with."

"So you're already doing that. What else? What haven't you done yet that you want to do?"

She furrowed her brow. "I wish now I hadn't given up racing."

"Why did you? Because you were afraid of getting hurt?"

She shook her head. "No. I think that was just an excuse."

"Then why?"

She worried her lower lip between her teeth. "My mother had been after me for a while to give it up." She ducked her head, but not before he read the hurt in her eyes. "She said it was selfish to waste so much time and energy on something I'd never be able to make a living at."

Cassie selfish? Admittedly, he didn't know her that well, but he couldn't picture her as selfish.

"You were really good. I remember."

When she didn't answer, he reached up and tucked a lock of hair behind her ear. "I'll bet you could still be good enough to race competitively."

She looked suspicious. "What makes you think that?"

"I have good instincts about people. You're not an ordinary person, no matter what you say."

"I guess it doesn't matter now," she said. "I'm past the age most racers make it big."

"That sounds like something somebody else told you."

She winced. "I thought about getting back into racing last year, but Bob didn't like it."

"Bob's a jerk. You want me to go down the hall and bust his chops?"

The beginnings of a smile pulled up the corners of her mouth. "It's tempting."

"I could let the air out of his tires."

She grinned. "We could put sugar in his gas tank."

"Or order room service and lace it with laxatives."

She giggled. That was better. He liked to see her smile. "We could sneak into their room and stick pins in all his condoms," she said.

"Ouch! You play rough, don't you?"

She made a face. "Yeah, that's me. Cast-iron Cassie."

She didn't look cast-iron. With her hair mussed from sleep, her cheeks slightly flushed, she looked soft and sweet...and oh, so tempting. The thought of anyone hurting her brought a rush of anger. "The guy's a loser." He cupped her face in his hand and turned her face to look at him. "You deserve better."

Her eyes met his, questioning. Challenging. "Do I?"

He knew words weren't the answer she wanted. And talking wouldn't be enough to express what he was feeling for this surprising woman who had literally burst into his life when he needed her most.

Their lips met and he thought he heard her sigh. Or maybe that was him, unable to keep silent in that first rush of release.

She pressed against him eagerly, tasting of champagne and strawberries. Her lips were soft as velvet, warm and pliant beneath his own. He opened his mouth and she followed his lead. Their tongues met, hesitant at first, then with more eagerness. He hadn't been wrong. Cassie was a woman of passion, made all the more powerful by the fact that she hid this side of herself so well.

He slipped his arms around her, pulling her closer. They kissed again, bodies fitted together as tightly as their lips. The hard points of her nipples pressed against his chest, and her heart pulsed in rhythm with his own. He'd been out of his mind to think he could resist a temptation like this.

He pulled back just enough to look at her. She flushed and ducked her head, as if suddenly embarrassed, but he put one hand beneath her chin and coaxed it up, until her eyes met his once more. "I'm glad you wandered in out of that snowstorm," he said.

She licked lips swollen from their kisses. "I...I'm glad, too."

He caressed her neck, then slid his hand along her shoulder. He wanted her out of this sweater, so he could see her naked beauty. But he didn't want to frighten her away. Better to take things slow.

"Guy?" Her voice was anxious, breathy.

"What is it?" He smoothed his hand down her arm.

She swallowed, her tongue darting out to lick at her lips, the gesture sending another jolt of desire through him. "Why don't we go into the bedroom?"

He froze, his hand on her wrist, and slid his gaze to hers. The raw desire in her eyes shook him. "If that's what you want," he said.

She smiled, and slid her hand up to twine his fingers in his. "Oh, it's what I want," she whispered. She stood and tugged him upright. "It's what I've wanted ever since I walked in that door."

5

Guy LET HER LEAD HIM into the bedroom, over to the bed, where she stopped to face him. Gaze still locked to hers, he pulled her into his arms and kissed her. The hesitancy of her earlier caress was gone, replaced by an urgency that shuddered through them both.

They kissed hungrily, tongues exploring, learning the contours of each other's mouths as if determined to make up for all the months and possibly years they'd been attracted to one another and never acted on that desire. He followed the line of her jaw with his mouth and kissed his way down the pale column of her neck. He wanted to explore every inch of her, but doubted he'd be able to hold himself back that long, at least this first time.

She surprised him again by taking the lead, tugging his shirttails from his pants and sliding her hands up his back to feel his bare skin. He smiled, and grasped the bottom of her sweater. "I don't think you need this anymore, do you?"

She laughed as he pulled the sweater up over her head. The silk of her lingerie brushed his knuckles and he turned his hand over and slid it up from her waist to cup her breast. He brushed his palm across the tip and she gasped in response. The sound sent a jolt of sensation through him. When he took her nipple between his thumb and forefinger, she squirmed against him. She was so wonderfully sensitive. Watching her made his own desire almost unbearable.

Still caressing one breast, he bent his head to suckle the other through the satin. The fabric brushed across the nipple with his tongue, magnifying the sensation. Cassie moaned softly as he flicked his tongue back and forth. He paid the same attention to her other breast, leaving two damp circles in the black satin.

He paused to catch his breath, and to look at her again. He couldn't get enough of looking at her, all that milk-white skin against the dark satin, that tangle of blond hair falling to her shoulders.

"What are you looking at?" she asked.

"Just enjoying the view."

She laughed, and reached for him, fumbling with the buttons of his shirt. He tried to help her, but she pushed his hand away. Finally the shirt front parted. She pulled him to her, pressing her damp breasts to his chest. "It's entirely too warm in here for you to be wearing so many clothes," she said.

"I could say the same for you," he said, pulling down the waistband of her pants.

Laughing, they began peeling off each other's clothes. He stopped her when she reached down to unsnap the teddy. "Leave it on for a bit."

She nodded, and he continued stripping to the skin, catching his breath as the cool air hit his fevered erection. The gasp changed to a groan as she reached out to stroke him. "I can see I'm not going to be disappointed," she said.

He pretended to be offended. "Did you really expect to be?"

Not waiting for an answer, he gently pushed her down onto the bed, onto her back, then he eased down beside her. He kissed her eyelids, her mouth, her neck, until his lips found the sweet, sensitive skin beneath her jaw. He pressed his mouth to her flesh and felt the strong beat of her pulse, pounding with the strength of her passion.

She traced the curve of his shoulder, fingers kneading his muscles, trailing to his hip, and the curve of his buttocks. She smiled as she squeezed him, as if relishing some secret joke. "Something amusing about my butt?" he asked.

She shook her head. "Only that it's one of the nicest rear ends I've ever seen."

She giggled, but he stifled her laughter with another kiss. Then, still pinning her with his mouth, he pushed down the straps of the teddy and peeled the damp satin away from her breasts.

He raised his head to look at her, and sucked in his breath. Her breasts were milky white, with rosy areolas and tight, erect nipples. He covered one with his hand, his own flesh dark against the paleness, the nipple tickling his palm. She arched toward him, pressing against him, filling his hand. When he took one nipple in his mouth, she let out a low cry of pleasure.

His erection was hot against her thigh, aching for release, but he refused to rush his own pleasure, or hers. He lavished attention on her breasts, first one and then the other, teasing them with teeth and tongue, massaging them with his hands until she squirmed beneath him, gasping with pleasure.

He cradled her against him, hands still, merely holding her, giving them both time to pull back from the edge a little. To think of all the times he'd seen her behind the coffee counter and had wanted to ask her out, but hadn't taken the chance. Why had he wasted so much time they could have spent together? He wouldn't make that mistake again. Some things were worth taking risks for, and Cassie was one of them.

CASSIE CLUNG to Guy, the way she might have clung to a lifeline to keep from falling into an abyss. Every nerve tingled, every inch of her felt more alive than she'd ever been before, and yet she wanted more. She needed more. She arched against him, the throbbing need within her building.

"Shhh." He smoothed his hand down her arm. "Take it easy for a minute."

But she hadn't found the courage to knock on his door in order to take it easy. This was her fantasy, her dream come to life, so she decided to do now what she'd only imagined doing before.

She caught him by surprise when she took hold of his erection. She knew by the way his eyes flew open and his breath caught. The knowledge made her smile. He was hot and heavy in her hand. She traced the length of the shaft with one finger and he twitched. "Careful there," he gasped. "It might go off."

"You think so?" She leaned over and swept her tongue around the base of it, the taut skin smooth as silk.

He groaned and his hand tightened on her shoulder. A thrill shot through her, knowing that she could make him feel this way. Guy Walters, the man who had starred in her every erotic daydream and late-night fantasy for the past six years, wanted *her*.

She looked up at him, into his eyes. "Let's not wait any longer."

She lay back, and he reached down to unsnap the fastening of the teddy at her crotch. A tremor shook her as his fingers brushed her sensitive center and she bit her lip to hold back a moan. He slid one finger inside her, advancing and retreating, her excitement building with each stroke. She panted, tightening around him, anticipating the release that would soon come. His finger left her and she cried out, reaching for him, but he put a comforting hand on her shoulder. "Soon, I promise," he said, and knelt between her legs.

She closed her eyes, waiting, tensed for the moment when he would fill her. Instead, he moved away.

"Shit!"

"What is it? What's wrong?" She sat up, heart pounding.

He sat apart from her, the picture of misery. "I didn't exactly come prepared for this," he said. "I mean...I don't have any protection."

Was that all? Relief flooded her. "I can take care of that." Evading his reaching arms, she slipped from the bed and retrieved her backpack from the other room. Carrying it with her back to the bedroom, she pulled the box of condoms from the outside pocket.

"Don't move." She looked back over her shoulder and saw that he was sitting up, grinning, gaze focused on her behind as she bent over the backpack. "There's a lot of great scenery up here," he said.

She threw the box of condoms, hitting him square in the chest, sending the plastic-wrapped packets flying. He fished one from his lap and stripped off the wrapping while she crawled back to his side.

"Allow me." She held out her hand and he surrendered the condom and lay back while she fitted it to his shaft. He started to sit up again, but she pushed him down. "Stay right there," she ordered, and straddled him.

He caught on to what she was after and grasped her hips to help guide her onto him. She closed her eyes as he filled her. Even in her imagination, it had not been this good, this right.

Slowly, she began to move, setting a rhythm for him to match. She kept her eyes open at first, watching the play of emotions on his face as his excitement built. One hand grasped her bottom, while the other hand found the center of her pleasure and began to stroke her. Gently at first, then with more pressure, he caressed and kneaded, until she threw back her head and moaned. "Come on, baby," he coaxed. "Let go."

She did let go, a free-fall leap that sent her soaring. She may have screamed. She knew she drove down hard on him, sending him to his own climax. They clutched at each other, moving together through the last spasm of release, finally coming to rest in each other's arms.

She closed her eyes, lips curved in what very well might have been a permanent smile. Something soft brushed her cheek and she realized Guy was kissing her—gentle, butterfly kisses that brought a rush of tears to her eyes. She had expected a lot of things from her reckless decision to seduce him, but she hadn't anticipated such tenderness.

She moved down, nestling her head in the hollow of his shoulder, not wanting him to see the tears. He'd likely think her crazy if he did. What kind of a woman throws herself at a man, then cries about it? How could she explain that her tears weren't a sign of regret, only an expression of her happiness?

She expected to feel guilty, but maybe that would come later. Right now, joy warmed her through. She closed her eyes and breathed in deeply, wanting to memorize the scent of sex and Guy and wood smoke. She traced her hand across his chest, determined to remember that sensation as a reminder that this had really happened. One time in her life, she had taken a chance. She had done something daring and turned fantasy into reality.

He kissed the top of her head. "That was incredible."

She smiled. "It was, wasn't it? Even better than I imagined."

"Oh, you imagined this, did you?"

She blushed. "I imagine a lot of women have fantasized about you."

"I'm not interested in a lot of women. I want to know about you." He eased her out of her arms and rolled over onto his side to face her. "So tell me about these fantasies. What did we do in them?"

She giggled, and stared down at the sheets between them. "I'll never tell."

"Come on, Cassie." He captured a lock of her hair

and twined it between his fingers. "I want to know. What turns you on?"

She shook her head, still avoiding his gaze.

"All right, why don't I tell you what turns me on and then you can tell me."

She didn't answer with words, but raised her head and looked at him expectantly.

He smoothed his hand along her shoulder, down her arm. "I'm turned on by a woman who's not afraid to go after what she wants. A woman who surprises me."

His searching gaze sent a tremble through her. "Do I surprise you?"

He rested his hand at the curve of her waist. "You've been one surprise after another. How many women would even think of erotic Scrabble?"

She laughed. "So you liked that?"

"I'll never look at those letter tiles the same way again."

He continued his explorations, moving his hand to her hip. "Come on, it's your turn. What turns you on?"

You was the simple answer, but maybe the real answer lay in what about him, about their situation, made her blood heat and her senses reel. "I think...an element of risk." She traced the contours of his chest with her fingers, along the breastbone, around the dusky nipple. "Not knowing what to expect."

"Uh-huh." He captured her hand in his own and kissed her fingertips. "What else?"

She closed her eyes and thought. "Certain smells turn me on." She put her nose close to his skin and inhaled deeply of the soap and sex and wood smoke scent. "And the way things feel." She freed her hand from his grasp and continued her journey down the plane of his stomach. "The sense of touch can be very erotic."

His breath caught as she stroked the skin below his navel. "You've got very, um, skilled fingers. Does that come from your massage therapy studies?"

"Maybe so." She caressed his stomach, and felt the muscles tremble.

"The way you're touching me now is certainly turning me on." he said.

"I want to touch you more."

"I want you to never stop touching me." He reached for her shoulders and started to roll her over onto her back, but she stopped him.

"Wait. I want to do something, something just for you."

"You've already done plenty for me."

Laughing, she slipped away from him, out of the bed and over to her pack. She returned with the bottle of massage oil. "I want to give you a massage," she said.

He grinned. "I'd be a fool to turn down an offer like that."

She instructed him to lie on his stomach while she warmed the oil in her hands. When she opened the bottle, the scent of cinnamon filled the air. "That smells good," he said.

"Mmm." She began to knead the muscles of his shoulders. His skin warmed beneath her hands, and she savored the feel of him. He had a gorgeous body, sculpted by a lifetime of athletic endeavor.

"That feels incredible," he murmured. His eyes were closed, a faint smile on his lips.

She knelt on the edge of the bed, putting her weight into her work. He snaked out an arm to clasp her waist, but she pushed him away. "Relax. Let me do the work."

He moved his arm away and grew quiet, but energy still hummed between them, the connection they'd forged in their lovemaking still strong.

She loved touching him this way, memorizing every knot of muscle or ridge of flesh. She moved down his back, along each vertebra to the base of his spine. She massaged his tight buttocks, and his muscular thighs, the edgy electricity of arousal adding pleasure to her work. Of course, usually massage wasn't an erotic experience. It could be healing, or spiritual, or intensely physical, but with Guy it was all those things and more.

She forgot about time, about the rest of the world or worries or anything else beyond this man on this bed in this moment. She forgot about everything, until his hand stopped her again. "You'd better stop. Now," he said, his voice strained.

She stilled, and he rolled over onto his side and pulled her down next to him. "It's your turn now," he said, and reached for the bottle of oil.

She laughed. "You don't have to do that."

"Oh, but I want to."

He was strong, but surprisingly gentle, not focusing so much on a traditional massage as a full-body caress. She closed her eyes and surrendered to his stroking hands. His fingers smoothed down her back and along her sides, teasing the sides of her breasts with a feather touch, then sliding down to her buttocks, smoothing and kneading, massaging away the last remnants of oil while stoking the fire within her.

She felt hot and liquid, need building within her. Guy bent and kissed the back of her thigh and she moaned softly. "Please...I don't want to wait any longer...."

He rolled her onto her back and stretched out beside her, but when she reached for him, he pinned her arms at her sides. "Shhh. You relax and let me do the work."

He skimmed his fingers down her stomach, across her thighs, then came to rest at the center of her longing, his hand hot and heavy. She arched against him, craving release.

Keeping his hand pressed against her, he took her nipple into his mouth and began to tease it with his tongue. She sucked in her breath and clutched at the sheets. "Guy, please," she panted.

He shifted his hand, dipping one finger into her. She shuddered, tightening around him. He rolled her toward him, and began to suckle at her other breast, while his thumb began to gently stroke.

She came quickly, powerfully, a keening cry of release torn from her. She curled toward him, reaching for him, wanting him more than she had ever wanted anyone. But still he held her off, his fingers continuing to stroke her, insistent, bringing her once again to the edge and over.

Then he was sliding into her, filling her completely, riding with her to that bliss. She opened her eyes, wanting to see him, watching as desire sharpened his features, then softened them again as his climax overtook him. Tenderness and joy mingled with a feeling of tremendous satisfaction. *She* had made him feel this way. Guy Walters, the man of her dreams, had wanted her more than anything at that one moment. The same way she had wanted him.

6

CASSIE WOKE MUCH LATER, to a darkened room. Guy lay on his back beside her, snoring softly. She smiled and closed her eyes again, courting sleep, but her stomach rumbled, prodding her more awake.

The clock read 12:13 a.m. when she slipped from bed. She found Guy's bathrobe on a hook on the back of the bathroom door and put it on. She paused to bury her nose in the lapel, savoring the scent of him that clung to the garment the way she was sure it now clung to her own skin.

In the kitchen, she switched on the light over the sink and rummaged for something to eat. Her search revealed a six-pack of beer, a package of jerky and another of summer sausage, cheese, crackers, mustard, a box of Frosted Flakes but no milk, and a king-size bag of tortilla chips. A typical man's idea of a weekend's provisions.

She settled for cheese and crackers and some of the summer sausage. She took the food into the living room and curled up on the sofa in front of the now-cold fireplace. The condo had the muffled quiet of late night dreams. Maybe this was a dream, after all.

In the world outside of dreams, she'd never be here, in Guy's condo, with Guy asleep in the next room. This

was a night she'd fantasized about, but never thought
to make into reality.

She reached for another cracker and bumped the picture of the Boulder Bandidos. She picked it up and
stared at the group of young men. The wild adventur-
ers, who would do anything and risk everything. And
Guy was their ringleader. The wildest and most
daring.

She stared at the handsome young man in the middle of the group, and thought of the older version of
this man who lay naked in the next room. Looking at
this picture made her heart pound and her stomach do
somersaults. And it made a treacherous voice in her
head whisper words like *love* and *forever*.

She put the picture back on the table and shoved the
rest of the food aside, her appetite vanished. Those
words terrified her. What did she know about love?
After all, she thought she'd been in love with Bob, and
for the two years they'd been together she'd put all her
dreams—all her life—on hold. Now that she was free
of him, here was her chance to live those dreams again.

Guy said he believed she could make those dreams
come true. That she could race again. And yet in one
night, he'd come dangerously close to making her forget about everything and everyone else.

She turned and looked out the window. The snow
had stopped and the moon shone like a spotlight on a
wedding-cake world. A fantasy world. Was she falling
in love with Guy? A person couldn't think straight
when in love. Or even in lust. No wonder some athletes
swore off sex when they trained. How was she ever go-

ing to get her life together if she had gorgeous Guy Walters filling up her thoughts—and her bed?

GUY DREAMED he was holding Cassie, caressing her satiny skin, reveling in the scent of her hair, kissing her...

He awoke tangled in the sheets, his arms wrapped around the pillow where Cassie had slept. The woman herself was across the room, fully dressed and stuffing what looked like the black satin teddy into her backpack. "What are you doing?" Guy sat up and threw back the covers.

She glanced toward him, then hastily looked away, a warm blush coloring her cheeks. "My friend Jill is on her way to pick me up. The storm's cleared and the roads are open again."

"But you don't have to leave." He stood and reached for her, but she slipped out of his grasp.

"Thanks for letting me crash here last night. I really appreciate it, but I've intruded enough and I really need to get back to Boulder. Jill said the shop's been really busy and I just remembered I forgot to water my houseplants. So I'd really better be going." She grabbed up the backpack and tried to push past him, but he blocked her exit.

"I wouldn't call it an intrusion at all," he said. "I said I was glad you walked through that door and I meant it."

She smiled, a sweet sexy expression that sent his blood pressure soaring. "I'm glad, too. Last night was..."

Last night was incredible. Erotic. Exciting. Endearing... "I thought this morning we'd pick up where we left off last night."

She looked startled. "Oh, no, that's impossible."

He looked down, at the part of him that was standing at attention, ready for action. "I'd say right now it's very possible."

Her blush deepened. "No, really, Guy, last night was a fantasy, a dream come true. You can't take a fantasy out into the real world."

He frowned. "You might think it was a fantasy, but it was one hundred percent real, flesh and blood to me."

She fumbled with the straps of the backpack. "I'm not doing this right. I had it all planned out what I would say, to make you understand, and I take one look at you and all the words fly right out of my head."

He moved to take her into his arms. "Then I'd say it's time we stopped talking." He pulled her close and kissed her, his mouth insistent, exploring, tasting, pleading with her to stay. When he finally released her, she was flushed and breathless. Apparently, he hadn't convinced her. She slipped on the backpack and grabbed her coat. Any moment now, he expected her to wave it at him like a matador's cape.

"Guy, we're two different people," she said. "It would never work between us."

This was really getting annoying. What did it take to convince this woman? "I don't agree. I think we're more alike than you realize."

She shook her head. "We are not. Look." She pointed to a photograph on the bedroom wall. It was a shot of him, rock climbing, taken two summers ago.

"That's you," she said. "Mr. Never-pass-up-a-dare. You like adventure, excitement, danger. You're extraordinary. Me, I'm ordinary. I lead a quiet, conventional life. One day with me and you'd be bored out of your skull."

"We've already spent a day together and I guarantee you, I wasn't bored. And I wouldn't exactly call what you did—coming up here bent on seduction—ordinary."

She avoided his gaze, and pushed past him toward the door. "That was a once in a lifetime thing. Like I said, a fantasy." She paused at the door to look back at him, eyes full of regret. "I can't live on fantasy. But thank you. I'll never forget last night." She blew him a kiss, then left him alone.

He started to follow, then realized he was still naked. Not that modesty took precedence over romance, but with the thermometer near zero, it wouldn't take long for important parts to freeze off. So he gathered the clothes he'd worn yesterday from the floor and shrugged into them, then shoved his feet into his boots and took off after her. By the time he reached the lobby, she was gone.

He searched the lobby area, hoping she'd slipped into some quiet corner to wait for her ride, but except for a few early-morning skiers and late, late partiers, the lobby and the area outside around it were empty. Feeling empty himself, he trudged back up the stairs.

He went through the motions of making coffee, hardly aware of what he was doing. His mind was too full of the events of the past eighteen hours, trying to absorb all that had happened. Despite his reputation around town as something of a playboy, he'd never made love to a woman he didn't know well before. He liked to date a girl a few times before he took her to bed. And yet, Cassie hadn't seemed like a stranger to him. Looking into her eyes, feeling himself inside her, it was as if he'd known her—really known her—all his life.

Cassie was right about one thing. In some respects, last night had seemed like a fantasy, a dream of how perfect it could be between one woman and one man.

He took a long drink of coffee and shook his head. Last night with Cassie hadn't been a dream, or a fantasy, or a figment of his imagination. It had been as real as anything he'd ever experienced, as real as the scent of her lingering on his skin, as real as this dull ache in his chest now that she was gone.

He set his coffee cup down on the counter and stared at his reflection in the toaster. He'd come here yesterday wondering what he was going to do with his life. Now he had his answer. He was going after Cassie Carmichael and he was going to make her his own. Heaven help anything, or anyone, who stood in his way.

"SO ARE YOU going to tell me what happened or do I have to play my collection of seventies bubblegum music until you cry uncle?" Jill glanced at Cassie, then downshifted and pulled into the passing lane.

Cassie stared out the window, at the piles of brown slush pushed over to the side of the road by the snowplows. "I told you, Bob came up here to spend the weekend with some hussy named Mary Ann Patterson."

"I think I know her. Short brunette, big boobs?"

Cassie nodded. "That's her."

"Her bank account's even bigger than her boobs. Her daddy owns Patterson Publishing."

"It figures Bob wouldn't go for some *poor* tramp."

"Uh-huh. So you saw them together and then what happened?"

"Nothing happened." Nothing but the most incredible night of her life.

Jill lowered her sunglasses and gave Cassie a skeptical look. "Don't lie to me, hon. You don't look like a woman who spent the night sitting up in the lobby. And if I'm not mistaken, that's a love bite on your neck."

Cassie's hand flew up to cover her neck. Jill laughed. "Gotcha! Now fess up. Did you meet somebody?"

She nodded. "Not just somebody. Guy Walters."

The car swerved. Jill brought it back under control and slowed. "You're joking, right?"

Cassie shook her head. "No. He was at the resort. In a condo on the same floor as Bob's."

"And you just happened to run into each other in the hall and he invited you in?"

"Not exactly." She sighed. She might as well tell Jill everything. Barbara Walters was an amateur interviewerer compared to Jill. When she wanted to know something, she wouldn't let up until you'd confessed to everything you'd actually done and some things you'd only thought about. "He didn't invite me in. I invited myself in."

"I don't think I'm getting the picture here. You—Miss I-haven't-asked-for-a-raise-in-two-years—just walked up to Guy Walters and invited yourself back to his room?"

"No, I knocked on his door and when he opened it, I walked in." Even now, she couldn't believe she'd done it, or anything that had followed. "I sort of seduced him."

The car swerved again, brakes squealing. Cassie held on as the car zoomed down the exit ramp and Jill whipped into a gas station. "Suddenly low on gas?" she asked.

Jill shut off the engine and turned to look at her friend. "I need you to explain that last statement. What do you mean, you seduced Guy Walters? How did you manage that?"

"We played Scrabble."

"Scrabble?"

She squirmed in her seat. "Well...sort of erotic Scrabble."

Jill started laughing and Cassie joined in. It did sound ridiculous now, but last night it had been a deadly serious game. "Erotic *Scrabble!*" Jill howled. "That is so...so...so you!" She wiped her eyes and shook her head. "So you really did the deed? You spent the night with Mr. Gorgeous?"

She nodded. And what a night it had been. She'd expected to be turned on physically, had hoped for passion, and then had been totally blown away by Guy's combination of tenderness and intensity. When he'd held her close and murmured her name, it had been so easy to pretend he really cared.

"I guess he didn't live up to your dreams, huh?"

Jill's question startled her. "What? No! I mean, yes. It was awesome. Incredible." She searched, but short of stopping to buy a thesaurus, she didn't think she'd find the words to do justice to what she'd experienced with Guy.

"Then why did you call me at six-thirty on a Saturday morning? You sounded desperate."

"I *was* desperate. I had to get out of there before Guy woke up and talked me into staying."

Jill pressed her fingers to her temples and closed her eyes. She opened them again and glared at Cassie. "Let me get this straight. You finally get it together with your dream man—a man half the women in college voted 'best tush in town'—and you can't wait to leave? What are you—crazy?"

She sank down in her seat. "Probably."

"And what exactly is your reasoning here? Are you, like, playing hard to get?"

She crossed her arms under her breasts. "Look, last night with Guy was great, but it was only a fling—a fantasy. We'd never last out in the real world. Why make ourselves miserable trying?"

"Bull malarkey! That's the lamest excuse I've ever heard." Jill leaned toward her. "What's really going on in that head of yours?"

She stared out the window. "I don't want a man in my life right now. After Bob..."

"Bob is a major bozo. Please don't tell me he's ruined you for all other men. That is so soap opera."

"It's not that, it's..." It would be so easy to lose herself in loving Guy. This weekend had convinced her she needed to work on getting her life in order. She planned to finish massage school and look out for her own interests for a change. "I've got to get my life straightened out. I don't need a man getting in my way."

"You need a shrink." Jill faced forward once more and started the car. "Talk about a fantasy—there's no such thing as getting your life together."

Cassie leaned her head against the car window and closed her eyes. She didn't have to own a crystal ball to see what would happen if she got involved with Guy. Like everything else in her life, it would start out great, then go downhill from there. She'd start worrying about pleasing him and forget about pleasing herself, the way she'd done with Bob. Or Guy would meet some adventurous, outdoorsy type, who'd be a better match for him. At least this way, she still had the memory of their one magical night together. For that one night, common Cassie Carmichael had been Cinderella, Wonder Woman and Xena, Warrior Princess, rolled into one. Now that she was back in the real world, she still carried a little of that magic with her. Maybe enough to change her life forever.

7

MONDAY STARTED OFF all wrong for Cassie. She slept through her alarm, probably because thoughts of Guy had kept her up most of the night. It was bad enough the man distracted her all day, the things he did in her dreams kept her hot and bothered most of the night.

She barged into work fifteen minutes late to find Jill inundated by the morning rush. She barely had time to say hello before she was up to her neck in grande lattes and tall cappuccinos.

Some time before ten, the onslaught of customers ended. Cassie wiped down the front counter while Jill restocked the pastry trays. "Have you thought any more about what you're going to do about Guy?" Jill asked.

The sound of his name made her stomach flutter. She shrugged. "There's nothing to think about. I'm not going to do anything. There's nothing between us."

"Uh-huh. Is that why you just poured salt into the sugar shaker?"

She looked down at the box of salt in her hand and the jar clearly labeled Sugar. "I didn't sleep well last night, that's all," she muttered. She emptied the jar into the sink and started over. This had nothing to do with Guy.

The bell on the door jangled and her stomach lurched. The *last* person she wanted to see walked in the door.

"Bob. What are you doing here?" Jill asked.

Bob sauntered to the counter and removed his wrap-around sunglasses. "Hello, Cassie, how are you?"

She turned her back to him. "I'm not speaking to you."

"Cassie, I came here to apologize. I know you're up-set with me, but honest, I can explain."

She rolled her eyes. "Just what do you intend to explain?"

"About Mary Ann. That was a mistake. I realize that now." He looked at his feet, and assumed an expression she thought of as his sad puppy dog face. This particular look had always melted her heart before, but now she remained unmoved. "This is hard for a man like me to admit," he said. "I need you, Cassie. You're the only woman for me."

"He means he needs you to pick up his dry cleaning and fetch his beer," Jill said.

Bob scowled at Jill. "Haven't you got some coffee to poison or something?"

"Jill, it's okay," Cassie said. "I can handle this." She turned back to Bob. "What about Mary Ann?"

He shrugged. "I'll admit she has money and she's hot-looking, but compared to you..." He shook his head. "Anyway, I know you're the only woman I'll ever love."

His eyebrow twitched like an electric eel—a sure sign he was lying. Cassie stared at him, amazed that she had ever found him desirable. Had she really wasted two years of her life with this loser? "You love beer. You love hockey. But you don't love me. You don't even know me."

"Aw, Cassie, come on now..."

The bells on the door jangled again. Cassie didn't pay any attention to the new arrival until Jill jabbed her in the side. "What?" She looked up and saw Guy. For a moment, she stopped breathing.

She'd forgotten how incredible he looked in person. He was dressed in a tan-and-white rugby shirt that emphasized his broad shoulders, khaki pants that showed off his muscular legs, and hiking boots. When he smiled, she felt warm all over, as if the room was suddenly flooded with sunlight.

"Hi, Cassie."

She picked up a towel and began polished the display case. She could sense Guy's gaze boring into her, but she refused to look up. "Jill, take Guy's order."

"Oh, I don't think so." Jill folded her arms and leaned back against the refrigerator.

"Cassie, have dinner with me." Guy put his hands on the counter and leaned toward her. "Tonight."

His cologne wafted around her, conjuring an immediate image of him naked, and the memory of their bodies pressed together. She shook her head, trying to clear it. "No."

"Just dinner. That's all. Please." His voice was soft, seductive.

She felt like whimpering, but she had to be strong. "No."

"She's not having dinner with you. She's having dinner with me." Bob sidled up to the counter again.

"We'll go to the Lobster Lagoon," he said. "Your favorite. I'll even spring for lobster." He paused, then added, "The tails. Not the whole one. I'm a little short right now."

"Gee, a big spender," Jill commented.

Cassie gave him a withering look. "Go away, Bob."

Guy loomed over Bob, muscles flexed. "You heard the lady. Leave her alone."

Cassie felt surrounded by testosterone. It was enough to make a woman giddy, but she reminded herself helplessness wouldn't do her any good. She forced herself to look at Guy. "You need to leave, too."

"Me?" He looked offended. "Why do you want me to go?" He took her hand in his. "We need to talk. We'll go someplace quiet. Romantic." His thumb stroked her palm, sending tremors through her. "How about the Flagstaff House?"

The Flagstaff House was the most expensive restaurant in Boulder, offering five-star service and a spectacular view of the city from its perch on the side of Flagstaff Mountain. And they had the most delectable chocolate mousse.... She shook her head, refusing to yield to the temptation of Guy or the mousse. "No. Absolutely not."

"Cassie, please," Guy coaxed.

"Give the man a break," Jill said.

"Cassie, listen to me," Bob demanded.

"What does a fellow have to do to get a cup of coffee around here?" This last from a gray-haired man at the front counter.

Jill went to wait on the customer while Guy and Bob argued over Cassie. She stood between them, their words swirling around her like so much steam. She put her hands over her ears to shut out their voices, but still they talked, punctuating their argument with her name.

Cassie. Cassie. Cassie.

What was she doing in this ridiculous situation? Did either of these men even care what she felt? What she wanted? Of course not. Why should they? She had never put her own feelings first in her life.

Except this weekend, at Aspen Creek. When she'd knocked on Guy's door, she'd put herself first. She'd shoved aside worries about what people expected of her or what they'd think and done something just for her. It had been an amazingly selfish act, and it had felt great.

"Shut up," she said.

No one paid any attention.

"Shut up," she said again, louder.

The two men stopped talking and looked at her. "Both of you, out!" She pointed toward the door.

"Cassie, I—" Guy said.

"Cassie, you—" Bob whined.

She stared at them, exasperated. "Fine, if you won't leave, I will." She ripped off her apron and threw it down.

"What are you doing?" Bob asked.

"I'm leaving." She collected her purse from its cubbyhole, grabbed her coat and pushed through the half door separating the counter from the rest of the shop.

"Where are you going?" Guy followed her toward the door.

"To live the rest of my life. If the two of you don't

like it—well, I don't intend to stick around to hear about it." With that, she was out the door, into the sunshine and traffic, into a freedom that both excited and frightened her. She hurried away from the shop, then began to jog, reveling in the sheer joy of moving. From now on, she was going to follow her own path. No more quiet, complacent Cassie. She was going to do what she wanted with her life and no man, not even Guy Walters, could stop her.

"YOU WANT TO DO WHAT?" Jill paused, a falafel wrap halfway to her mouth, and stared at Cassie.

"I'm thinking about quitting my job at Java Jive to go to massage therapy school full-time." Cassie avoided Jill's gaze, pretending to hunt for another morsel of chicken in her Chinese chicken salad. Two days had passed since her confrontation with Guy and Bob at the coffee shop, and she'd spent most of that time thinking about the future. Her future.

She'd hoped lunch at their favorite spot along Boulder's Pearl Street pedestrian mall would put Jill in an agreeable mood. From their seats next to the window, they could watch the parade of shoppers, tourists, students and itinerant musicians who strolled the outdoor mall.

But today, Jill wasn't easily distracted. She laid aside her wrap. "What exactly would you live on?"

Cassie pushed aside a piece of lettuce with her fork. "I have some money saved. Not much, but enough."

Jill picked up her wrap again. "And this doesn't have anything to do with wanting to avoid seeing Guy Walters?" She took a bite.

"Of course not." She saw Guy every night in her dreams, anyway. "Guy and I are friends. I don't have to avoid him."

Jill nodded. "Uh-huh. You and Guy are friends the way the Beatles were just a little rock group. You know he wants you and for some reason, that scares the living daylights out of you."

"I'm not scared." Except of having her heart broken. A girl had a right to protect herself, didn't she?

Jill finished off the last of her falafel and licked her fingers. "Don't you think it's odd that this new determination to make something of yourself comes *after* your mind-blowing night with Guy Walters?"

Cassie shifted in her chair. "I was thinking about all this before that night. It's why I went to Aspen Creek in the first place." Though she had to admit, if only to herself, that her night with Guy had given her the courage to go after all her dreams—at least the most practical ones.

Jill looked thoughtful. "I think you're trying to distract yourself from Guy. Maybe *he's* the only real change you need."

"Who are you all of a sudden, Dr. Laura?" Cassie picked up her tray and carried it to the trash can.

Jill followed. "All I'm saying is that the hunkiest hunk in town is gaga over you and all you can do is talk about your sudden desire to give back rubs to naked strangers. Does that make any sense?"

"That's not fair. Massage therapy is about a lot more than naked back rubs." A sudden warmth flooded her as she remembered the back rub she'd given Guy.... She pushed the mental image away. "As a massage therapist, I could really help people. I've been looking for something like this a long time." Maybe even since college. When her friend Amy had been injured, she'd wanted more than anything to help her. "As a massage therapist with a specialization in sports medicine, I can help people recover from injury."

Jill looked contrite. "I'm sorry. You're right. And I'm sure you'll make a great massage therapist. But that doesn't mean you have to put the rest of your life on hold."

Cassie shook her head. "I've been letting everything—and everybody—get in the way of this too long. I think it's time I concentrated on doing this one thing—for me." And that was all she wanted to say on the subject. She didn't want to think about Guy, and she certainly didn't want to talk about him. The only way to get over him was to put him out of her mind as much as possible.

She scraped the remains of her lunch into the trash and left the tray on a folding stand. "Let's stop by Caribe Clothing Company and see if that dress I want is on sale."

"Stop trying to change the subject." Jill hurried after her. "What are you going to do about Guy? Why won't you even give him a chance?"

Because I think I'm already in love with him and it would hurt too much to lose him. Better to never really have him. She didn't dare say those words aloud. Instead, she stopped and faced Jill. "What Guy and I had wasn't real. It was...make-believe. Fantasy. Like dressing up like wenches and knights for the Renaissance Festival, or going on vacation to some city where no one knows you and doing all the things you'd never do at home. It was fun, but it wouldn't last."

"How do you *know* that?"

She sighed. "Because, I've spent half my life trying to manipulate impossible situations, pretending to be happy when I'm not. I'm not going to do it anymore."

"What *are* you going to do?"

"Right now, I'm going to Caribe Clothing Company to buy a dress."

Jill fell into step beside her as she headed down the mall once more. "Get pink. I hear that's Guy's favorite color."

8

"TELL ME EVERYTHING you know about Cassie Carmichael." Guy leaned over the counter and watched his sister, Amy, attach plastic antitheft tags to a stack of bright cotton shirts. Amy was three years younger and six inches shorter than Guy, but when they were children, people had sometimes mistaken them for twins. They had the same dark hair and blue eyes, and the same adventurous spirit.

"Who?" Amy paused in her work and looked up at her big brother.

"Cassie Carmichael. Cute blonde. The two of you went to high school together. Were on the ski team at CU. I seem to remember you were pretty good friends."

Amy's mouth tightened into a thin line. "We were friends. But that's a long time ago. I have no idea what she's up to now."

"She's working at Java Jive and studying to be a massage therapist."

Amy jerked her head up, surprise barely masked by annoyance. "If you know all that, why are you even asking me?"

"Because I want to know more. What happened between you two, anyway? Why aren't you friends anymore?''

Amy turned away and busied herself neatening a stack of knit shirts. ''I don't know. We drifted apart. People do.''

Guy frowned at the back of his sister's head, a funny feeling in his stomach. It wasn't like Amy to lie to him. ''That was about the time you both left the ski team, wasn't it?''

''I had to quit because of my knees. She just gave up.''

Guy winced at the bitterness in her voice. He put a hand on her shoulder, intending comfort, but she jerked away, and moved over to a display of dresses. He shoved his hands in his pockets and stayed where he was. ''Okay, so you haven't seen her in a while. What was she like before that? When you were still friends?''

Amy stilled, as if really considering the question. ''She was kind of quiet.'' She looked over her shoulder at him. ''Not your type.''

''I never said there was anything wrong with quiet women. Not that I've known any before.''

She swatted at him, but he dodged out of the way. ''You've certainly never dated any,'' she said.

''I want to date Cassie. So tell me about her.''

There. He'd said it. He'd see what Amy had to say about it now.

Worry lines fanned out from around her eyes. ''Why would you want to date her? Don't you have enough women running after you?''

''I like her. I mean, I liked her before, when you two

were only a couple of kids, but now I like her even more."

She shrugged and looked away. "What difference should it make to me?"

"I'm not asking your permission, I'd just prefer to have you on my side here."

"I don't have anything against Cassie. I just don't particularly admire quitters."

"You're wrong. Cassie's not a quitter."

"You hardly know her. How can you say that?"

"I just know." The woman who'd spent the weekend with him had been strong and tenacious—not the type to give up easily. "When Cassie left the team, she must have had a good reason."

Amy shrugged. Obviously, she wasn't going to let go of her grudge that easily. Still, he couldn't let Amy's feelings keep him from Cassie. They'd been friends once. He could help them be friends again. "So tell me about her."

She gathered up the shirts and shoved past him. "Why are you asking me? Seems like if you want to date a woman, you ought to at least know *something* about her. I mean, you didn't pick her name out of the phone book, did you?" When he didn't answer right away, she glanced back over her shoulder at him. "Did you?"

He shook his head. "She's not listed." He followed her to a display at the front of the store. "We met up at Aspen Creek last weekend. She followed this jerk she was dating up there and caught him with another woman."

Amy began arranging the shirts on the display rack. "Where do you come in?"

He pretended to be looking through a display of brightly colored overalls. "She needed somebody to talk to, and we sort of ran into each other and, well, one thing led to another."

Amy groaned. "Don't tell me Cassie Carmichael is yet another on your long list of conquests."

"Maybe the last on the list."

He had her there. She didn't even bother closing her mouth after a gasp escaped her. She dropped the last of the shirts and reached up to cover his forehead with her hand. "You don't feel feverish." She stood on tiptoe and stared into his eyes. "Your pupils aren't dilated." She frowned. "Or is that constricted pupils?"

"What are you talking about?" Guy tried not to laugh.

"I saw it on *ER.* This man was suffering from delusions and had all these weird symptoms."

"I am not suffering from delusions."

"You're sure suffering from *something.* You've never talked like this about any woman."

"I'm thirty-one years old. Why are you so surprised I'm ready to settle down?"

Amy shook her head. "I guess I've always pictured you as the playboy type."

"Then you've pictured wrong."

Amy returned to straightening the shirts on the rack. "Mom and Dad will be glad to hear it. They've already started dropping hints about wanting grandchildren."

The thought of having babies with Cassie made his

stomach flutter. "What about you? Don't you want a husband and kids?"

She shrugged. "Someday. I'm in no hurry."

Guy frowned. Come to think of it, Amy didn't seem to date much. Why was that? He started to ask her, but she spoke first.

"Why Cassie?"

"Cassie's special."

She frowned. "I don't know, Guy. From what I remember, Cassie isn't the type to stick with any one thing for too long. How do you know things between you two will be any different?"

"I just know." How could he explain the way Cassie had touched not only his body, but his soul, in the short time they'd been together? She'd made him really *feel* things, and helped him see his life in a new light. He knew it wasn't logical to think about love after one night with a woman, but for the first time in his life, that's exactly what he was thinking.

"Tell me what you remember from school," he said. "What did she like or dislike?"

Amy shook her head. "Sorry. I really don't want to talk about Cassie." She returned to the counter and opened a second box of merchandise. "Oooh, now these are nice." She held up what looked like fluorescent boxer shorts.

Guy leaned on the counter. "Come on, sis, I need your help here."

"Sorry, lover boy, your love life is your own business." She tossed a pair of the shorts to him. "Here, try this on."

The fabric rustled in his hands, stiff and crinkly. "What is it?"

"It's a swimsuit. Come on, try it on. You'll look great in it."

He frowned at the bright-pink-and-green garment. "If this was all I had to wear, I'd just as soon go skinny-dipping." He tried to return the trunks to her, but she crossed her arms over her chest.

"Try it on and I might be persuaded to talk more about Cassie."

He didn't know how much help that would be, but right now he was looking for any clue that would help him get Cassie's attention. "Okay."

A few moments later, he emerged from the dressing room wearing the multicolored swim trunks. He frowned down at himself. "This isn't really my style. I look like I've been in a paintball fight."

"You look great," Amy said. "We should have you model a pair in our next fashion show."

"In your dreams. I wouldn't be seen in public in this ridiculous getup." He tugged on one leg. "This makes me look silly."

"Now you know how women feel when they try on swimsuits. Walk around a little for me."

"You'd better hope no one I know sees me." He took a few steps out into the aisle.

The front door swung open, letting in noise from the mall, and Cassie Carmichael.

Her hair was windblown and she had a spot of what looked like mayonnaise on her sweater. Guy thought she had never looked better, unless of course, he counted the times he'd seen her naked. "Hi, Cassie," he said.

Eyes wide, she stared at him. "Oh, my!" she breathed, as a pink flush washed across her face.

AT FIRST, Cassie thought one of the images from her nighttime dreams had made its way into her day-dreams. How else to explain being confronted with a naked—or nearly naked—Guy in the aisle of a clothing store? The bright swim trunks he wore only empha-sized his flat stomach, long legs, tight buttocks and, um, other manly attributes. She tore her eyes away from those attributes and looked up, only to be met by a heart-stopping smile that held both welcome and in-vitation. "Like my new swimsuit?" he asked.

"Don't wear it to the pool, you'll start a riot." Jill stood beside Cassie, obviously enjoying the view, as well.

"What are you doing here?" Cassie finally found her voice.

"Looks like he's shopping," Jill said.

"My sister, Amy, manages this place." Guy jerked his head toward the back of the store.

"I'll come back later." Cassie turned to leave, but Jill blocked her exit.

"Oh, no, I'm staying to shop," Jill said. "And we're in my car, remember?"

She thought about leaving anyway, and taking the bus home. Anything to get away from Guy's perfect body and that inviting smile. Before she could move, he grabbed her arm and pulled her toward the back of the store. "Come say hi to Amy."

Amy Walters shared her brother's dark good looks, though her features were more delicate. Her seeming fragility was deceptive, however. She'd been a daring skier, never afraid to try the most difficult trails or brave the most dangerous conditions. Cassie had been more naturally talented, but also more cautious. In the end, those differences in temperament had come between them.

Cassie smiled hesitantly. "Hi, Amy."

"Hi, Cassie." Amy didn't smile. She folded her arms across her chest. "Haven't seen you in a while."

"Yeah. It's good to see you again."

Cassie felt about two inches tall when Amy looked away. Obviously her old friend still had hard feelings. Just as well she'd put a stop to things with Guy. The last thing she wanted was to be the cause of a family feud.

She glanced at Guy. He was frowning at his sister, fingers clenching and unclenching as if he was fighting the urge to shake her.

"Can I help you find anything in particular?" Amy asked.

Cassie looked away from Guy. He was only a man. A gorgeous, perfect man with whom she'd spent one incredible night—but still, only a man. "Uh, yeah. I saw a dress in here before that I liked. Sort of long, pale yellow with green embroidery."

"Sure, that's right back here."

The only way to get to the dress was to brush by him. She pretended not to notice him as their bodies touched, but the heat that swept across her cheeks betrayed her. "So, Cassie, what have you been doing?"

he asked, following her and Amy to the back of the store.

She shrugged. "Nothing much. Working."

"She's thinking of enrolling in massage therapy classes full-time," Jill called from the front of the store, where she was rifling through a stack of shorts.

Cassie narrowed her eyes at her friend. Jill grinned and stuck out her tongue.

Need any volunteers to practice on? She waited for the line, but it never came. "Massage therapy's pretty popular these days," he said. "A lot of physical therapists are prescribing it for muscle injuries and strains."

Cassie rewarded him with a smile. "That's what I've been trying to tell Jill, but she keeps getting it confused with some kind of sex job."

"Uh-huh." His gaze locked on to hers and she caught her breath. Who was she kidding? The massage she had given him had been *all* about sex.

"I think this is the dress you wanted." Amy brought out a yellow knit dress embroidered with green flowers.

Cassie took the dress and held it against her. "What do you think?"

"It's one of our most popular styles," Amy said. "Why don't you try it on?"

"I will." She disappeared into the dressing room.

To her astonishment, Guy followed her. "I need to get out of this swimsuit," he explained, and ducked into the curtained alcove next to hers.

She began to undress, conscious of him moving around on the other side of the wall. He was probably

naked by now, the swimsuit discarded, leaving him totally unencumbered...

"Cassie?"

His voice, so near, startled her. "Yes?"

"Have you ever made love in a dressing room?"

"N-no." Her heart pounded. What had prompted
such a question? Was he propositioning her? What did
it say about her, that she was tempted to answer yes?

"Neither have I, but I'm beginning to see the possibilities." His voice was low and smooth, caressing her.
"It's such a small, intimate space. Well lit. With a
mirror."

Her nipples stood at attention against her thin camisole. She covered them with her hands, as if she could
ease the aching. Damn Guy Walters! It ought to be il-
legal for any one man to be so sexy. "You're only saying that to distract me," she said.

"Is it working?"

She could hear the laughter in the words, and smiled
in spite of herself. "Yes!"

"Good. Then have dinner with me Friday."

"I can't."

"Why not? A woman's got to eat."

"I have a class."

"A massage therapy class?"

"Yes. We have our first practice session with volunteers that night."

"Then how about Saturday?"

She shook her head. "No, Guy. We'd better not."

"But—"

"Guy, will you get out of there and stop harassing
my customers?" Amy's voice drifted over the parti-

tion. Cassie was grateful for the curtain to hide her blush. She'd forgotten for a moment that there was anyone else in the store.

"Goodbye, Cassie." He paused outside her dressing cubicle. "It was nice undressing with you."

She laughed. What a terrible, wonderful flirt Guy was. Too bad they hadn't started out as friends instead of lovers. She could have been his friend, without risking losing her heart.

OUTSIDE THE DRESSING ROOM, Guy paused to catch his breath. Things had been heating up there for a while. He'd even begun to think he was winning Cassie over, and then she'd turned him down cold when he'd asked her to dinner.

Jill sidled up to him and held out a pink minidress. "What do you think of this, Guy?"

He glanced at the dress. "I think Cassie would look great in that."

Jill laughed and looked at Amy. "He's got it bad, doesn't he?"

Amy scowled. "He's got something, all right."

"Why do women do that?" he asked.

"Do what?" Amy adopted her patented innocent look.

"Why do you analyze men and talk about us as if we're not even in the room?"

"Why do men say and do so many things that simply beg to be analyzed?" Amy smirked at him and darted behind the counter as he moved to envelop her in a bear hug.

"Watch it there, *little* sister," he said. "I'm still bigger than you."

"Uh-huh. Bigger and *slower*."

The dressing room curtain fluttered and Cassie stuck out her head and one bare shoulder. "Yellow doesn't look right. Do you have the same dress in blue?"

"Sure," Amy said. "I'll get it for you."

Guy focused on where Cassie's shoulder had been, but she'd already disappeared back into the dressing room. Maybe Amy was right. A man had to be pretty bad off to get turned on by something as innocent as a woman's bare shoulder.

He looked around and spotted Jill over by a rack of swimsuits. Hands in his pockets, trying to look casual, he sauntered over to her. "So, what does Cassie say about me?"

Jill looked him up and down. "What makes you think she says anything about you?"

"Come on now, I know women talk."

"How do you know that?"

He glanced around them, then leaned closer. "Because *men* talk," he said.

She shook her head. "I think telling you anything would be against the rules."

He frowned. "What rules?"

"The best friend rules." She ticked them off on her fingers. "Never sleep with your best friend's boyfriend. Never borrow her clothes if they look better on you. Never order dessert when she's on a diet. And never talk about her behind her back."

"Come on. I don't want you to say anything bad about her. I just want to know what she thinks about me."

A Mona Lisa smile tugged at Jill's lips. "Well...she *did* mention that she ran into you this weekend."

Ran into him. That sounded pretty casual, didn't it? "And? Is that all she said?"

Jill plucked a purple-and-green bikini from the rack and studied it. "I think she said something about... playing Scrabble?"

"Scrabble. Yeah, we played Scrabble." He'd never look at those letter tiles in the same way again. "And that's all she said?"

Jill burst out laughing. "What do you want to hear? That she told me the two of you had the sheets smoking? That you were absolutely the best man she'd ever had in bed?"

His face reddened. Not that he didn't like hearing he was good, but... "Did she really say that?"

Still laughing, Jill shook her head. "No."

"Oh." His shoulders sagged. So their one night together really hadn't meant anything to Cassie.

"She didn't say it, but she didn't have to," Jill said. "I could tell by looking at her."

He glanced back toward the dressing room, where Cassie was accepting the blue dress from Amy. "Then why did she run away from me? And why does she refuse to have anything to do with me now?"

Jill replaced the swimsuit on the rack and sighed. "She says she needs to concentrate on other things right now. Plus, she thinks the two of you have nothing in common. That she's not adventurous enough for you."

"That Scrabble game was pretty damn adventurous." He folded his arms across his chest. "Besides, I'm ready to settle down. Why won't she even give me a chance?"

"Cassie's kind of a complicated person. She's quiet and she looks and acts pretty ordinary, at least most of the time. But there's a lot going on inside her head." She put a hand on Guy's arm and lowered her voice. "To tell you the truth, I think she's afraid."

"Afraid?" He frowned. "Of me?"

"More like afraid of herself." She shook her head. "She's been hurt. She doesn't trust her own instincts anymore."

Cassie emerged from the dressing room, blue dress in hand. "I'll take it," she told Amy.

Guy turned back to Jill. "I really like her. I mean it. I'm not going to hurt her."

Jill patted his arm. "Don't give up yet. Be persistent and I think you have a chance of getting through to her." She smiled. "I'm rooting for you."

Persistent. He could handle persistent. Persistence had gotten him to the top of twenty of Colorado's fifty-four fourteeners—peaks over fourteen thousand feet. Persistence had helped him make Mountain Outfitters one of the most successful businesses in Colorado.

Persistence would help him find a way to Cassie Carmichael's heart.

9

CASSIE HAD NEVER thought about how difficult it would be to avoid a man she actually *liked.* For the next week, every time she turned around, Guy was there: at the dress shop, at the coffee shop, on the street. When he wasn't with her in person, he was filling her thoughts. A whiff of CK One cologne would stop her in her tracks and have her craning her neck in a crowd, hoping to spot him. Every time she made a breve mocha, she thought of him, and he had taken the innocence out of dressing rooms forever.

Now here she was in class, trying to listen to a lecture on pressure points, and her mind kept wandering to Guy. *Snap out of it!* she ordered herself. This class was important to her future, and that future did *not* include Guy.

"Tonight, we have a group of volunteers on whom I want you to practice the basics we've learned about reflexology." Their instructor, an earnest woman named Mo, moved toward the classroom door. Her Birkenstocks slapped against the tile floor as she walked. "Volunteers, please come in," she said as she opened the door. "Find a student and take a seat in the chair in front of them."

A grandmotherly woman in a blue sari headed toward Cassie, who smiled and stood to welcome her. But a man darted ahead of the woman and slid into the chair at Cassie's station. A tall, dark-haired man with Mel Gibson-blue eyes. "Hello, Cassie."

"Guy, what are you doing here?" She kept a smile on her face, though her eyes telegraphed her annoyance. She didn't think arguing with a volunteer would add points to her grade.

"I'm volunteering for a massage." His suggestive smile was turned up all the way. "I thought it'd be a good way for us to get to know each other better."

Cassie looked around, hoping to see the grandmotherly woman or some other unclaimed volunteer. But everyone had found a partner. Mo spotted her and glided over. "Is something wrong?"

"No. Not at all." Cassie picked up her towel and sat. "Guy, I'm going to give you a foot massage."

Guy sat, though the expression on his face showed he was clearly disappointed. "A foot massage?"

Cassie stifled laughter. "That's right. No naked on the table this time. Now take off your shoes."

He bent and began unlacing his boots. "I put on clean socks, just for you."

"Start with the right foot," Mo instructed. "The first thing you should do, students, is become acquainted with the shape of the foot."

Grinning, Guy offered up his right foot. Avoiding his gaze, Cassie positioned it on the towel on her lap and lightly traced her fingers around its contours. It was a large foot, with a high arch, a well-shaped heel and long toes lightly dusted with dark hair. Like everything else about him, Guy had very sexy feet.

"The foot is one of the most sensitive, and sensual, parts of the body," Mo said. "As we have discussed, the practice of reflexology is based on the premise that certain areas in the feet correspond to every part of the body. Problems or ailments in other parts of the body may be addressed through the feet. Thus, you always want to ask your client if he or she is having difficulty with any other part of their body before you begin their foot massage."

Cassie assumed a neutral expression and looked up at Guy. "Are you having any problems with any areas of your body?"

He grinned. "Not problems, exactly. Unless you count sexual frustration."

She ignored him and poured a small amount of almond oil into her hand. "A foot massage is supposed to be very relaxing. The book reports some people even fall asleep while having their feet massaged."

"Fat chance of that."

She stroked her thumb along the arch of his foot. The skin was smooth and she could feel the muscles beneath. "This area of the foot is associated with the colon," she explained. She moved to the ball of the foot, exerting more pressure. "And here is linked to the lungs."

He shifted in his chair and she looked up, alarmed. "Did I press too hard?"

He shook his head. "I'm ticklish."

"How are we doing over here?" Mo leaned over them. "My, what a nice large foot you have Mr....?"

"Walters. Guy Walters."

Mo put a hand on his shoulder. "You have very nice

feet, Mr. Walters." She smiled, her gaze silently approving the rest of him, as well. "Thank you for volunteering for our class."

"My pleasure," Guy said.

Did every woman in the world have to ogle him that way? Cassie frowned and concentrated on applying pressure to the ball of his foot. She had the smug desire to inform her teacher that yes, it *was* true what they say about men with big feet, or at least *this* man.

She poured more oil into her palm and began working on the top of his foot, smoothing her thumbs across it in long, sweeping strokes. Guy watched her through half-closed eyes. "I love having your hands on me," he said.

She flushed. "I'd look pretty silly trying to give you a massage without using my hands."

"Oh, I don't know. It might be fun to try some time. Warm up some oil and try spreading it around with everything but our hands."

Warmth flooded her and she didn't dare look at him. She swallowed hard and tried to focus on her work. "We've been practicing using long, strong strokes, like this." She pushed the ball of her thumb along his instep.

"That feels good. I never knew touching could be so erotic."

How could touching Guy be anything but erotic? Especially considering that every time she was near him, she remembered the one incredible night they'd spent together?

She glanced up and found his eyes on her, his gaze smoldering with a desire that took her breath away. "I wish we were alone in this room right now," he said softly, below the clamor of the other students and volunteers that surrounded them.

"B-but we're not alone." She glanced around them. Everyone else was absorbed in their own work, not paying attention to her and Guy.

"No, but if we were, I'd be touching you, too. Turning you on the way you're turning me on right now."

She swallowed again. "Uh, Guy, I get graded on this."

He smiled. "I'd give you an A plus."

She shifted in her chair, fighting arousal. What kind of person got turned on giving a *foot* massage, for goodness sake?

Guy wriggled his foot forward, until his heel was resting firmly against her crotch. Warmth spread through her, along with embarrassment. She tried to move, but that only succeeded in creating more pressure in exactly the right place. She glanced up at Guy. He was watching her through half-closed eyes. "Stop it!" she hissed.

His lips formed the beginnings of a smile. "Do you really want me to stop?" He shifted his foot again, sending delicious sensations skittering through her.

"Guy, we're in *class*," she pleaded, struggling to control her breathing.

"That's part of what makes it exciting, don't you think?" He moved again, and she had to dig her fingernails into her thighs to keep from moaning.

"All right now, let's switch to the left foot," Mo instructed the class.

Cassie sighed with relief as Guy withdrew his foot

from her lap, but her reprieve was short-lived. Now he arched his left foot toward her most sensitive spot. "Guy, please," she gasped. Who would have thought a man could have such talented toes?

"You don't know what it does to me, watching you," he said.

She raised her head and met his eyes, the force of his look pressing her back in her chair. His gaze roamed over her, caressing her neck, fondling her breasts, stroking her thighs with all the effectiveness of a physical touch. And all the while, his foot continued its gentle pressure.

"Do you still want me to stop?" He grew still, waiting for her answer.

She looked into his eyes, and realized this moment wasn't about him proving a point or forcing her into an uncomfortable position. He would stop if she asked him to.

The old Cassie would have asked him to. That Cassie would have worried what people would think, would have told herself nice girls wouldn't take such risks, no matter how good it felt.

She glanced around the room. The other students and volunteers were absorbed in their work. Even Mo was busy demonstrating some technique to a student at the front of the room. She looked back at Guy, at the desire in his eyes, desire for her. "Don't stop," she whispered. She closed her eyes, surrendering herself to the thrill of his touch, made all the more intense by the possibility that they might get caught.

His movements were steady and relentless, the sensations building until she gripped the sides of the chair, panting. Her climax overtook her in a rush, sending tremors through her and warming her to her toes. She clenched her teeth to keep from crying out, but still a gasp escaped her. When she opened her eyes, Guy was smiling at her. "Best foot massage I've ever had," he said.

She returned the smile, and turned her attention once more to his foot. Could she help it if her strokes now held an extra measure of tenderness?

"You'll want to wrap it up now, class," Mo called. "Volunteers, when you're done, please collect one of these evaluation forms to fill out. You can drop them in the box in the lobby."

Cassie wiped excess oil from Guy's foot with her towel. "I guess you'd better go now," she said.

"Uh, it's not exactly safe for me to stand up yet." She noticed then that he'd draped a towel over his lap.

She covered her mouth with her hand to hide her smile. "Why don't I move over here while you put on your shoes?"

"No, wait." He leaned forward and grabbed her wrist. "Have dinner with me tomorrow."

She bit her lip to keep from saying yes. As much as she wanted to be with Guy, tonight proved how much he was capable of distracting her. "I don't think that's a good idea," she said.

"Why not? You won't make me believe you're not attracted to me."

She raised her eyes to meet his, silently pleading for understanding. "It's because I *am* so attracted to you that we shouldn't get involved," she said. "I can't afford that kind of distraction right now. I have to finish my schooling and figure out what I want to do with my life. And I can't do that and juggle a relationship, too."

He set his mouth in a stubborn line. "People do it all the time."

She shook her head. "I've tried before and it didn't work."

He took her hand in his. "That's because you never tried it with me."

She shook her head. "No. I'm sorry. I really am." Grabbing her reflexology chart, she headed for the front of the room.

"Is everything all right?" Mo approached her, frowning.

"Oh. Yes. I'm just..." She resisted the urge to look back at Guy, focusing instead on the chart in her hand. "I'm a little confused about the best way to treat a neck pain. Could you explain it to me again?"

By the time Cassie returned to her chair, Guy was gone. She gathered up towels and replaced the cap on her bottle of oil, humming to herself. "How did you do?" the plump redhead who sat next to her asked. "Do you think you'll get a good grade?"

"I hope so," Cassie murmured. Tonight was just another session in class, but she felt like it had been a important test of her resolve to stay away from Guy. In the end, had she passed the exam, or failed?

GUY COLLECTED his bike from the rack in front of the massage therapy school. The ride home would help him calm down and unwind. He hadn't intended to end up in such a compromising position with Cassie, but when he'd sensed her growing arousal, it had seemed only natural to offer her some relief. And then he'd become so turned on himself....

He shifted on the narrow bicycle seat, still far from comfortable. If he didn't stop thinking about her, he was going to need more than exercise and a cold shower.

He stopped for the light at Broadway and Pearl and spotted the sign for the Bear's Thumb Brewpub ahead. He'd stop in for a beer, and unwind a little bit before he headed back to his apartment.

The Bear's Thumb had been designed to resemble a hunting lodge, complete with massive beams criss-crossing the ceiling, a moss rock fireplace large enough to roast half a cow, and bighorn, elk and mule deer mounts staring down from the corners of the room. A crowd had gathered at one end of the pub's front room to watch the Colorado Avalanche game on a wide-screen TV. Guy ordered a pint and took a seat at the bar, turning on his stool to take in the game. This was what he needed to get his mind off Cassie—a little down time, hanging out with other men.

"Hey, Guy, you're just the man I've been looking for."

The person who spoke was *not* someone Guy had expected to see again any time soon. Cassie's old boy-friend, Bob Hamilton, settled onto the stool beside him. "Hey, man, let me buy you a drink." He signaled the bartender and ordered refills.

Guy drained his glass and pushed it aside. "The last time I saw you, we were arguing over the same woman. Why would you want to buy me a drink?"

"Why should I have hard feelings about that? I can't blame you if we have the same tastes in women."

Guy winced. He didn't want to be reminded.

"Besides, I thought maybe you could give me some advice."

Yeah, like don't get within a mile of Cassie or I'll make sure you regret it. "What kind of advice?"

Bob accepted a fresh beer from the bartender. "Oh, you know. About women." He twisted the top off the beer. "Apparently, you've got something of a rep with the chicks. Not that I can't hold my own in that territory, but it doesn't hurt to pick up a few pointers." He raised the beer in salute. "It's us against them, after all."

Guy sipped his beer and waited to see what other words of wisdom Bob would feel compelled to share. What had Cassie ever seen in this man?

"So, what are your thoughts on this whole romance thing?" Bob helped himself to a handful of pretzels from a basket on the bar.

Guy raised one eyebrow. "Romance thing?"

"You know, chicks. They want the whole hearts-and-flowers thing. Men like you and me, we'd rather cut to the chase. Skip the frills, get naked and get after it."

Guy's hand tightened on the bottle and he tried not to think about how much he wanted to plant his fist right in Bob's mouth.

It would only be wasted effort anyway.

What if I told you I'd slept with Cassie? he thought. *Or that we just had an intimate encounter involving massage oil?* He glanced at Bob. The man reminded him of an Irish setter he'd had as a kid. Big and dumb.

"I mean, what do women want, anyway?" Bob asked.

The age-old question. "That's one I haven't figured out yet," Guy said.

Bob sipped his beer, his brow furrowed. "Their brains must work differently from ours," he mused. "I mean, I tried the direct approach, you know?"

Guy stared, afraid to ask what Bob's idea of the direct approach was.

Of course, Bob told him anyway. "I made it plain she was welcome in my bed anytime."

Was this Mary Ann, or some other lucky woman? Guy decided he didn't really want to know. "I take it that didn't go over too well."

Bob began peeling the label from his beer bottle. "Like I said. She wants the hearts and flowers. Romance first. Sex later."

Guy winced. And what had *he* been doing, in perhaps a less crass way? "I guess the direct approach isn't always the best," he said.

"Yeah." Bob wadded up the remains of the beer label and tossed it into an ashtray. "A buddy of mine said he thinks women want all that stuff they read about in romance novels—you know, flowers and candlelight and all that stuff."

Flowers and candlelight. How long had it been since he'd used that approach with a woman? After all, this was the twenty-first century. Modern women didn't really expect all that froufrou, did they? Modern women knew what they wanted and went after it, just like Cassie had invited herself into his room that evening, with her champagne and French lingerie.

But maybe Cassie, and other twenty-first-century women, appreciated doing things the old-fashioned way sometimes.

"What kind of flowers does Cassie like?" he asked Bob.

Bob frowned. "Why are you asking about Cassie?"

"Just...for an example. You know...what worked with her should work with another woman."

He nodded. "Oh, I get it. Well, let's see. Don't most women like roses?" He shook his head. "Damn, those things are expensive, though."

Guy thought roses were too ordinary for Cassie. "What other flowers does she like?"

"Sometimes she'd buy flowers for herself. Those frilly white things—daisies, I think."

Daisies. A sweet and innocent flower for a sweet and innocent woman. He nodded. "What kind of candy does she like?"

Bob laughed. "What else? Chocolate. I swear, you'd think it was some kind of drug, the way she went after it. I used to tell her she'd better watch it or all that chocolate was going to end up on her hips."

Guy hid a smile. "I've got to hand it to you, Bob, you've got a way with women."

Bob straightened and looked smug. "Some of us are naturals. I guess that's the way to handle it, then. A few flowers, a little chocolate...my worries will be over."

The Avs scored a goal and cheers rose up around them. Guy laid a five on the bar and clapped Bob on the shoulder. "Thanks for the beer," he said. "See you around."

He got on his bike and turned down Broadway. If he hurried, he had time to get to the late-night florist before Bob finished his drink. He'd show Cassie he could be as romantic as the next man. Well, more romantic if Bob was her basis for comparison. In any case, he'd convince her she didn't have anything to fear from him. He wanted to support her dreams, not keep her from them. Flowers and candy were as good a place to start as any.

10

"DON'T LOOK NOW, but somebody's getting flowers, and I'll bet a double mint mocha it isn't me." Jill stood on tiptoe to see over the espresso machine and out the front window of the coffee shop. A minute later, the door opened and a man in a Fran's Flowers T-shirt came in carrying an arrangement of red roses. "Is there a Cannie Carmichael working here?" he asked.

"That's Cassie. Cassie Carmichael," Cassie said.

The man glanced at the card. "Looks like Cannie to me, but it's your name, so I guess you know." He held out the flowers. "Here you go."

"Who are they from?" Jill slid over to her, eyes alight. "Read the card. Read the card."

Cassie set the vase on the counter and unpinned the card from the ribbon. Her heart was racing. Had Guy really sent her roses? And what did it mean if he had?

She slid her thumb under the envelope flap and popped it open, then drew out a handwritten card. *I'm the only man for you. Bob.*

Jill was up on her toes again, trying to see over Cassie's shoulder. "You don't look too thrilled," she said.

Cassie handed her the card. "They're from Bob."

"Bob?" Jill read the card. "What's this 'I'm the only

man for you' crap? Isn't it supposed to be 'you're the only woman for me'?"

Cassie picked up the vase and headed toward the trash can. "Either way, the man's delusional."

"Wait, wait." Jill snatched the vase from her hands as she was preparing to toss it in amongst the coffee grounds and sugar packets. "Just because they came from a creep doesn't mean we can't enjoy them. It's not every day we get roses around this place."

Jill put the rescued roses on a table by the window while Cassie tried to think what she'd say to Bob when he called. And he *would* call. He wouldn't miss the chance to brag about his generosity and gloat over his supposed conquest. He probably thought all it took was a few flowers to send her running back to him.

"Uh-oh. Now this is interesting."

Cassie followed Jill's gaze out the window and her spirits plummeted. A second florist's van was parked in the loading zone and a woman in a pink smock was headed their way.

"Bob must be desperate if he's spending that kind of cash on you," Jill said.

"Is there a Ms. Carmichael here?" The woman was almost hidden behind an arrangement of bright pink, orange and white flowers.

"I'm Cassie Carmichael." Cassie stepped from behind the counter to accept the arrangement.

"What kind of flowers are those?" Jill asked.

"Daisies and passion flower." The delivery woman smiled. "The customer was very specific." She winked. "You are one lucky lady. I tell you, if I was ten years younger..." She waved and walked out the door.

Jill and Cassie exchanged glances. "That sure doesn't sound like Bob," Jill said.

"No, it doesn't." Cassie unpinned the card from the ribbon and brought it to her nose. Was her imagination working overtime, or did she detect a whiff of CK One? She opened the card and read:

The daisies are for your sweetness, and because I heard you like them.

The passion flowers are for the passionate side you keep hidden most of the time, but I know it's there.

Both sides of you are dear to me.

Guy

A lump rose in her throat and she blinked back tears. Who would have guessed Mr. Adventure had this sensitive side? Was there anything about the man that wasn't perfect?

"I can tell by the gooshy look on your face that they're from Guy." Jill leaned closer. "Am I right?"

Cassie nodded. "You're right." She tucked the card into her pocket. This one she'd keep, and read again and again.

"Then they deserve a place of honor." Jill moved the vase to the front counter. "I tell you, I'm jealous. Two men never sent me flowers."

"I don't know why. I haven't done anything to encourage them." Not unless you counted having sex with Guy's foot. But she hadn't *said* anything to him...

The bells on the door jangled and a stocky man in a gray suit came in. "A grande iced latte," he ordered.

He leaned across the counter and addressed Cassie. "Did anyone ever tell you, you have the most beautiful eyes?"

She blinked. "Uh, not lately," she said.

The man laughed. "Well, you do. A pretty girl with pretty eyes." He accepted the coffee from her, paid the bill, then stuffed a five dollar bill into her tip jar. "Have a good day, beautiful," he said as he departed.

Cassie stared after him. "Must be hormones," Jill said. "All that frustrated desire. Men can sense it."

Cassie flushed. "I don't know what you're talking about."

"Oh. So you're telling me the sight of Guy Walters in those swim trunks the other day didn't get you all hot and bothered?"

Cassie turned and began wiping down the flavoring bottles. "Guy *is* a very handsome man."

"Yeah, like Alaska is a big state. If a man like that wanted me, I wouldn't bother playing hard to get."

The ringing phone interrupted them. Jill reached for it. "Java Jive, where the coffee's hot and the atmosphere is cool." She made a face and held out the receiver. *It's your mother*, she mouthed.

Cassie took the phone. Her mother never called her at work. "Hello, Mom. Is everything all right?"

"That's what I called to ask you. That nice young man of yours phoned this morning to let me know how worried he is about you."

Nice young man? Had Guy called her mother? "What are you talking about? What nice young man?"

"Why, Robert, of course." She heard running water, and pictured her mother standing at the sink in the kitchen of her Indian Peaks townhome. "He says you broke off your engagement."

She gripped the receiver so hard her knuckles ached. "Bob and I were never engaged."

Dishes clattered in the sink. Her mother had a perfectly good dishwasher, but she refused to use it, saying the only proper way to wash dishes was by hand. "Maybe not formally, but we all knew one day you two would get married. So what happened?"

Cassie rolled her eyes at Jill. "I suppose Bob didn't bother to mention to you that he was seeing another woman?"

"Now, dear, you know how men are. Why, your own father—"

"I don't want to hear this!" She began to pace. "Mom, I don't want to marry Bob. I don't want to marry anybody. At least not right now."

"Cassandra Lee Carmichael, listen to yourself." Her mother made a tsking sound. "You make it sound like marriage is a bad thing. I happen to think it's a wonderful institution."

"I guess so. You've been married three times."

"Exactly. If I didn't believe in it so much, I wouldn't keep trying."

"I'll keep that in mind, Mom. And one of these days I probably will get married. But not yet."

"Now, Cassie." Her mom's voice took on a coaxing tone. "It's time you looked in the mirror and recognized that you are twenty-eight years old. How many chances do you think you're going to have to get married and settle down?"

Cassie shut her eyes. "Twenty-eight is not old, Mother."

"I was nineteen when I married your father and twenty when I had you."

And twenty-three when you divorced, and twenty-four when you married husband number two. And thirty-two when you married number three... For May Petrovski Carmichael Rogers Sanderson, being without a man was the worst fate that could befall a woman. Even a philandering lowlife was better than living alone with only a daughter for company.

"I want grandchildren while I'm young enough to enjoy them," May continued. "And I know Frank would make a wonderful grandfather."

"So are you and Frank definitely getting married?" Cassie saw her chance to change the subject.

"Oh, I'm sure we will, as soon as his divorce is final. But I didn't call to talk about me. What are you going to do about Robert? He told me this really touching story on the phone about how you used to cook dinner for him every night and how much he misses that."

"He misses the food, Mom. He doesn't miss me."

"You know they say the way to a man's heart is through his stomach. My second husband, Darryl, always said he married me for my cherry-fudge cheesecake."

Cassie sighed. "Mother, I really don't want to discuss this right now."

"I'm merely trying to keep you from making a mistake you'll come to regret." More water running. "I knew you'd never confide in me. You keep things to yourself too much. That's part of your problem. And you're so flighty. How do you expect to attract a man that way?"

Why did her mother have to make romance sound like a fishing expedition? "I've got to go now, Mom. We have customers waiting." She punched the off button before her mother could protest, and laid the phone on the counter.

"Well." Hands on her hips, Jill confronted her.

Cassie drummed her fingers on the counter. "Bob called her. He told her I broke off our *engagement*."

"He called your mother and lied to her?" Jill let out a low whistle. "He must want you back in a bad way."

"I don't *want* him to want me." She slumped against the counter. "I want him to leave me alone."

"I think if you were openly dating Guy, Bob would get the message." She held up her hand. "I know, I know, you keep saying things with you and Guy wouldn't work out, but I don't believe it."

"The only thing Guy and I have in common is sex."

Jill grinned. "Sounds like a good start to me." She opened the pastry case and took out a fist-size brownie. "Care to drown your sorrows in a little chocolate?"

She nodded and Jill plopped the brownie on a plate and stuck it in the microwave. Cassie poured coffee for them both and tried not to think about what her mother had said. True to form, however, May's words had implanted themselves firmly in her brain. *You're too flighty. How many chances do you think you're going to get?* How could a man like Guy, who was so successful and adventurous, remain true to a woman like that?

Jill clinked her coffee cup against Cassie's. "To you and Guy."

Cassie tensed. "There is no me and Guy. There won't be a me and anybody until I finish massage therapy school and get settled."

Jill's eyes widened in mock horror. "They make you take a vow of celibacy to get your diploma?"

"Look, how many other things have I tried before this? College, real estate school, secretarial school. And every time I let something distract me from my goal—my mother, or worries over money, or Bob." She hugged her arms across her chest. "I won't let that happen this time. I really want to do this, and if that means swearing off men for the duration, I'll do it."

"I think it's really great that you have a goal, but isn't this approach a little extreme?" Jill propped her elbows on the counter, watching Cassie in the mirror behind the flavoring rack. "Still, I suppose there's always the old-fashioned way to deal with that kind of frustration."

"What, saltpeter?"

"I was thinking more of taking matters into your own hands, so to speak."

Cassie felt her face grow hot. "I don't—"

"Oh, come on, don't tell me you've never done it. You know all that stuff about making you go blind isn't true." She winked. "Of course, I do wear contacts."

"Of course I've...done that. But I don't talk about it." She glanced around. Thank goodness, the shop was empty. "Especially not in public."

Jill laughed. "You sound like 'good old Cassie' again. Whatever happened to being daring and adventurous?"

Cassie shook her head. If Jill only knew just how adventurous she'd been lately, she'd never believe it.

"I know what you need," Jill said. "You need a little mechanical friend."

"A what?"

"A vibrator. You have heard of vibrators, haven't you?"

"Of course I have, but that doesn't mean I need one."

"Yes, you do." Jill straightened. "Tomorrow I'm taking you shopping."

"Tomorrow's Saturday. I have a class."

"Only in the morning, right?" Jill grinned. "I'll pick you up at one."

GUY HAD DEBATED calling Cassie and asking how she'd liked the flowers. Did she think the note he'd written was too corny or weird? Did she think he was trying to bribe his way into her affections? In a way, that was exactly what he was doing, but that was beside the point.

In the end, he'd decided calling would make him look too desperate. He settled for riding by Java Jive on his bike and looking through the window to see that the flowers had indeed arrived. Unfortunately, all he saw was a huge arrangement of roses. He thought of the conversation he'd had with Bob. Could he... He shook his head. Nah. After all, Bob had left Cassie for Mary Ann. Maybe the flowers were for Cassie's friend Jill.

Now he was waiting outside the massage therapy school for class to let out. He'd pretend to casually run into Cassie and the subject of the flowers was bound to come up. From there, he could move on to step two of his plan, which called for a romantic dinner, with chocolate for dessert.

He checked his watch. Five after one. Class had been over since one o'clock. Where was Cassie? He scanned the men and women gathered at the bus stop, and checked the commons area where others had stopped to chat. No sign of Cassie. How could he have missed her. Unless...

He tapped a young Asian man on the shoulder. "Excuse me. Is there another entrance to this building?"

"Sure. Around on Ninth Street."

Guy cut across the lawn to the other side of the building. He arrived in time to see Cassie walking away with Jill. He stopped when they turned the corner onto Canyon. What was he going to do now? He couldn't very well romance a woman with her best friend as an audience.

He started walking, keeping Cassie in sight. Maybe she and Jill would split up before too long and he'd have his chance.

The two women made their way along Canyon, pausing to study the window display at a dress shop. They stopped at the corner of Canyon and Broadway and appeared to be arguing about something. Guy moved closer, hoping to hear what they were saying, but the light changed and the women crossed. Jill took Cassie's arm and led her into a shop on the east side of the street.

Guy followed, and paused outside the shop they'd entered. A sign over the door identified the place as Just 4 Play. A placard in the window advertised a special on body jewelry. He read the advertisement with alarm. Was Cassie planning on getting a tattoo or a na-vel ring?

The scent of patchouli enveloped him as soon as he crossed the threshold. A woman wearing a very small bikini offered him a tray of condoms.

He blinked, and realized the "woman" was actually a life-size blow-up doll. Next to her stood a mannequin in a leather corset, a pair of handcuffs dangling from her wrist. He spotted Cassie and Jill at the front counter, talking to a clerk with a pink Mohawk and a nose ring. He drifted closer, pretending an interest in a display of oils and lotions.

"Can I help you ladies?" the clerk asked.

"Um, we're just looking around." Cassie stared at a shelf of how-to manuals, her cheeks flushed pink.

"This is her first time," Jill explained. "She's a little nervous."

The clerk nodded. "We get a lot of first timers in here. But hey, sex is perfectly natural. Now what can I show you ladies today?"

"She's interested in a vibrator."

Guy almost dropped the bottle of strawberry-scented bubble bath he'd picked up. He moved over, until he could see the two women reflected in the mir-ror behind the counter.

"I'm really not sure—" Cassie began.

"We have quite a few models to choose from. Let me show you—"

"No!" Cassie put out her hand to stop him. "I've changed my mind." She looked around, frantic, then grabbed a bottle from a display by the counter. "I'll just take this."

"Cassie!" Jill frowned at her. "There's no need to be embarrassed."

"I can't help it, I am." Cassie opened her purse. "I just want to get out of here before anyone we know sees us." She handed the clerk her credit card, and kept her eyes on the counter while he processed her payment and wrapped up her purchase.

"Enjoy." The clerk grinned and handed her the package.

Cassie grabbed the sack and whirled around, crashing into Guy. He took her arms to steady her, and was in no hurry to let go.

She stared up at him. "What are you doing here?"

He reached over and plucked a box of condoms from the shelf. "Doing a little shopping."

"Glow in the dark, huh?" Jill nodded toward the box. "You wild man, you."

He grinned at Cassie. "Did you get the flowers?" he asked.

"Y-yes. They were beautiful. Thank you." She ducked her head. "The card was very sweet."

"I'm trying to be more romantic," he said. "I even borrowed some of my sister's romance novels."

"Did you learn anything?" Jill asked.

He shrugged. "To tell the truth, I got so caught up in the stories, I forgot to take notes."

She rewarded him with a hint of a smile. He nodded toward the bag in her hand. "So, what are you doing here?"

She blushed. He loved watching her do that. "Oh, you know…shopping."

His grin broadened. "What did you buy?"

She clutched the bag to her chest. "Oh, just...things."

"Let me see." In one deft move, he slipped the bag from her hand and took out a bottle of chocolate-flavored massage oil.

"I, uh, needed it for class." She took the bottle from him and dropped it back in the bag. "We're, uh, we're studying aromatherapy massage."

"Chocolate should be good for that. Of course, my personal favorite is cinnamon."

"Yes, cinnamon is nice." She looked as if she was trying very hard not to smile, and she continued to avoid his gaze.

"Maybe I could help you try out the chocolate sometimes. Just for the sake of comparison."

"Uh, we really have to go now." She looked around and spotted Jill, who was flipping through the how-to manuals. "Jill, we have to go," she called.

"What's your hurry?" Jill replaced the book and smiled at Guy.

"We have to go. Now." She grabbed Jill's hand and tugged her toward the door.

"It was nice seeing you both." He held up the box of condoms. "Guess I'd better pay for these."

The women said goodbye and left. Guy stepped up to the cash register. "If you shine a flashlight on these first, they look really cool," the clerk said.

"Do you personally test all the merchandise?" Guy asked.

The clerk grinned. "It's one of the perks of the job." The clerk handed him a jar from a nearby display. "Here's my favorite new product."

Guy read the label on the jar. "Body chocolate."

"Tastes great," the clerk said. "When you're not using it on your girlfriend, it's good on ice cream, too."

"I'll take it." Guy set it next to the box of condoms. After all, Cassie liked chocolate, didn't she?

"DIG A HOLE and bury me right here," Cassie said. She and Jill were waiting for the light at Broadway and Canyon to change so they could cross.

"Oh, that wasn't so bad," Jill said. "The clerk was really nice and they had a lot of neat merchandise."

"I don't care about that." She looked at her package. "Now Guy knows I've been in a place like that. A sex shop." She crossed her arms under her breasts. "Maybe I can leave town and change my name."

"Big deal. He'll think you're this incredible, liberated, wild woman." Hands on her hips, Jill faced Cassie. "Aren't you trying to change your image? No more little Miss Mouse? I mean, isn't this what you want?"

She didn't want to be a mouse, but that didn't mean she wanted to be a tiger, either. She just wanted to be...herself. Whatever that meant. "I don't know what I want."

"Except Guy. You want him."

"Yes, but..." But she didn't want him *now*. "I need time."

"Time for what?" The light changed and the two friends crossed the street.

"I need time to figure out what I'm doing and where I'm going. I don't need a man confusing me."

"I guess I can see how a man like Guy could be distracting. Just don't take too much time, okay?" Jill glanced at her.

Cassie nodded. How much time did she need? Enough to decide if she was strong enough to risk letting Guy into her life. Could she do everything she wanted to do and have a great relationship with a man like Guy at the same time?

11

THE HEART-SHAPED BOX of chocolates was as big as Cassie's dining table. She arrived home the following Wednesday afternoon to find it waiting on her doorstep and one look at the pink net roses covering the cardboard top made her queasy. She didn't have to read the card to know the chocolates were from Bob. Where he was concerned, tacky excess won out over tasteful restraint every time.

She had to tip the box sideways to get it through the front door. Once inside, she slid the box onto the table and contemplated it while she took off her coat. Was there really chocolate inside, or was the box a hiding place for something less pleasant, like rubber snakes or dog poop?

She hunted in the kitchen drawers until she unearthed an old chopstick, then used it to nudge the lid from the box. No snakes exploded from it. No sickly smells stung her nose. Instead, the contents appeared to be...chocolates.

She plucked the envelope from the top of the box and read Bob's note.

Sweets for the sweetest. Eat these and come to your senses. You know we were good for each other, Babe, so stop playing hard to get.

She wadded up the note and launched it toward the trash can. It missed and rolled into the corner by the re-frigerator. "You're a real romantic, Bob," she said aloud.

She selected a chocolate from the box and popped it into her mouth. It tasted of stale artificial flavorings, about what she'd expected from a cheapskate like Bob. Still, cheap chocolate was better than no chocolate. She leaned over the box again. *Now which one of these looked like a caramel...?*

The doorbell rang, startling her into dropping the newly plucked caramel onto the floor. She tiptoed to the door. If that was Bob, he could wait out in the hall all night for all she cared.

She put one eye to the peephole and let out the breath she'd been holding. Guy Walters leaned for-ward to press the bell again. Dressed in tight jeans and a leather bomber jacket, his hair windblown and falling across his forehead, he looked handsome enough to make a woman forget all about good sense. She jerked open the door. "Guy! What are you doing here?"

"I came to bring you this." He held out a small box wrapped in gold foil.

"For me?" She took the box, entranced, then men-tally shook herself. Just because Guy had more class didn't mean he could bribe his way into her affections any more than Bob could. She attempted to look stern. "How did you know where I live?"

"Jill told me." He leaned against the doorjamb, per-ilously close, the bomber jacket parting to reveal a T-shirt stretched tight across his chest. "I was ruthless.

I refused to stop buying her mocha frappacinos until she gave me your address."

"So she sold me out that cheap, huh?" She couldn't quite hold back a smile.

Guy leaned closer, his voice low, seductive. "Do you want me to leave?"

An evening alone with Guy, or a night in front of the television with a box of cheap chocolates? She held the door open wide. "Come on in."

He followed her into the apartment, his eyes surveying the living/dining/kitchen area. "It's not very big," she said. On her salary, she was lucky to afford a closet in Boulder's expensive housing market.

He paused before a framed pencil sketch of a ballerina she'd purchased at a flea market. "I like it," he said. "It's simple, yet feminine. Like you."

Was he referring to the sketch or the apartment? She ducked her head and studied the ribbon on the box. It was one thing to be alone with him in Aspen Creek in a snowstorm, quite another to have him here in her home. She took a deep, calming breath, but instead of the vanilla candles she burned to scent the rooms, all she could smell was the faint aroma of Guy's cologne.

He came to stand beside her. "Aren't you going to open your gift?"

She turned the box over and over in her hand. "Why did you bring me a gift?"

"Does a man have to have a reason to give a gift to a beautiful woman? Go on, open it."

Did flattery come so easily to him because he meant it, or because he was so practiced in delivering it? She tore the ribbon from the box and peeled back the paper, then lifted the lid to reveal a small jar of what looked like fudge sauce.

She removed the jar from the box and read the label. "Body Chocolate." She looked at him. "What does that mean?"

His laugh was low and throaty. "What do you think it means?" He traced his finger along her jaw. "It's chocolate you put on your body. And then someone licks it off."

She swallowed, the memory of Guy's tongue in intimate places making it hard for her to breathe. "Wh-why did you buy me this?"

"I heard you like chocolate."

She backed away, wanting space to breathe, to think, but he moved even closer. "I bought it at Just 4 Play, when I met you there Saturday. I thought we could try it out on each other."

She blushed. "I...I don't think that would be a good idea." She backed up again, until the sofa blocked her retreat.

"Why not?" He moved closer still, the front of his jacket brushing against her breasts. "I've been thinking about what you said, about our night in Aspen Creek being a fantasy." He kissed her jaw, his lips hot and moist. "Maybe what we need is to spend a night together in the real world, to prove that what happened between us wasn't a fluke." His tongue traced a path down her neck, sending a current of desire rushing through her. "That we can make the same kind of magic in the real world."

She might have whimpered. She certainly wasn't capable of more coherent speech. Every nerve was aware of him, responding with heated urgency. He put his arms around her and pulled her close, his mouth moving back up to her ear. "Don't say no. I want you too much."

How was a woman supposed to resist that kind of sex appeal? And why should she even bother? Here in his arms, she forgot every reason she'd come up with before. She put her arms around him and brought her mouth to his, kissing him for all she was worth.

He urged her onto the sofa and stretched out beside her. "Thinking about you has been driving me mad," he said, beginning to unbutton her blouse.

"I've been a little crazy myself." She ran her hands up under his T-shirt, reveling in the feel of his chest.

He tried to push her shirt back over her shoulders, but there wasn't enough room to maneuver on the narrow sofa. "I've got a better idea." She sat up. "Let's go into the bedroom."

She took his hand and led him into her bedroom, wondering if she was doing the right thing. Making love to Guy in a condo at a ski resort had been the stuff of fantasy, but bringing him into her own room... She paused in the doorway and he slipped his arms around her. She leaned back against him, closing her eyes, surrendering. He'd said he wanted to test out their relationship in the real world. Well, here it was, cotton flannel sheets and all.

He peeled back her shirt, kissing her bare shoulders, her back, trailing kisses down her spine. Still working from behind, he unfastened her bra and cupped his hands around her breasts. "Cold?" he asked, as the nipples hardened at his touch.

"Mmm." Not looking at him, she pulled off her jeans and panties and dove for the bed.

He met her on the other side, his discarded clothes forming a trail across the room. "So, have you tried out the chocolate massage oil?" he asked.

She flushed. "Uh, no." In fact, she'd shoved the bottle, still wrapped in the paper bag, into the nightstand drawer as soon as she'd gotten home. She knew she'd never be able to look at it without thinking of Guy.

"Why don't we save it for later?" He picked up the jar of body chocolate. "I think we'll stick to this." Unscrewing the lid, he scooped up a fingerful of the fudgy sauce and swirled it around her breast.

"It's cold!" Her giggles turned to gasps as he lowered his head and began licking off the chocolate.

"H-how does it t-taste?" she asked.

"Delicious." He raised his head and kissed her, a searing, chocolate kiss that put any gourmet sweet to shame.

When he broke off the kiss, she sighed, but the sigh turned to a moan when he transferred his mouth to her other breast. The satiny texture of the chocolate and the wet heat of his tongue combined to push her to new heights of arousal. "Guy, what are you doing to me?" she gasped.

He raised his head and smiled at her. "I'm making love to you. The way I've wanted to ever since you walked out of my condo at Aspen Creek." He moved lower, kissing his way down her stomach, across her thighs, and reaching once more for the jar of chocolate.

She laughed, ticklish as the cool chocolate dripped onto her, then caught her breath as he bent to taste. He slipped his hands beneath her, bringing her closer, and she jerked in response, almost incoherent with need. She clutched at the familiar soft cotton sheets and opened her eyes to stare up at the antique glass globe of the light fixture. Sunlight streamed through the curtains, falling across the bed and burnishing Guy's head with gold.

What had happened between them before had been the stuff of fantasy, but this...this was real. Guy was here, in her arms, in her bed. Before wasn't a fluke. Maybe they could make each other happy....

She cried out as her climax shook her, a deep, shuddering release that left her weak and gasping. Guy slid up to lie beside her, and stroked her cheek. "I should have you for dessert more often," he said.

She laughed and threw her arms around him. "What am I going to do with you?" she asked.

"How about this?" He rolled over onto his back, taking her with him. Grasping her hips, he guided her onto him. She sighed as he filled her, and began to move in a rhythm as natural as breathing. She stared down into his eyes, willing him to keep them open so she could watch as desire claimed him.

His eyes darkened, his expression almost fierce. He grabbed her and pulled her to his chest, so that she could feel the strength of his climax pulsing through them. Afterward, they lay silent for a long while, breathing heavily, too sated to move or speak.

Did this change things between them? She pushed away the thought. She didn't want to think right now.

She only wanted to hold on to this feeling, this moment. To imprint it on her brain and body forever.

Ding-dong!

Cassie opened her eyes, sure her imagination was playing tricks on her. Who would be ringing her doorbell *now*?

Ding-dong!

She raised up on her elbows. "Guy, someone's at the door."

"Ignore it. They'll go away." He smoothed his hand along her hips and squeezed the back of her thigh.

"Oh. All...all right." She collapsed against his chest, his continued gentle stroking erasing all thought of ever getting out of bed.

Unfortunately, or perhaps fortunately, he didn't render her deaf. As she lay back against the pillows, lost in a fog of renewed desire, she heard the distinct sound of the door opening and footsteps crossing the floor.

"Guy! Someone's inside my apartment." She shook him roughly, her heart pounding in panic.

He raised his head and listened as the steps moved toward the kitchen. "It's a burglar," Cassie whispered.

He looked at her. "Does anyone have a key? Bob?"

"No! I never gave him a key."

He looked thoughtful. "Now that's interesting. You date a man two years and you never gave him a key to your apartment?"

"He would have lost it, anyway." She shoved him away from her and reached for her robe, which hung from the post at the foot of the bed. "It must be Jill. You stay here and I'll get rid of her."

Instead of Jill, however, she found her mother waiting for her in the kitchen. "Oh, there you are." May looked up from the box of chocolates, a telltale smear of brown on the side of her mouth. "I rang the bell, but you didn't answer."

"Mother, what are you doing here?"

May ignored the question. "Are you ill, dear?" She marched over to Cassie and put a hand to her forehead. "Your face is all flushed and you do seem a little warm."

She'd been more than warm a few minutes ago, before she was interrupted. "Mom, I'm fine. I was uh...getting ready to take a shower."

"A shower? It's only six-thirty."

"I'm going out."

May brightened. "Is he anyone I know?"

"I'm going out with friends, Mom. *Girl*friends."

May shook her head and sat down on the sofa. "I can see I have my work cut out for me. I don't understand it. Where did I go wrong?"

Cassie tightened the sash on her robe and sat on the other end of the sofa. "Mother, what are you doing here?" she asked again.

"I came to talk to you about your love life. Or sad lack of one."

Cassie frowned. "You make it sound like I've never had a date."

Her mother waved away her protest. "I'm worried about you, dear. I thought I could help you."

"Mom, I'm not like you. I don't need a man to make me complete."

May scooted over and patted Cassie's thigh. "It's all

well and good to put up a brave front, dear, but I'm your mother, I can tell you're not happy."

Of course she wasn't happy. Her mother had just interrupted one of the most mind-blowing lovemaking experiences of her life. "I'm fine, Mom. Now, I really need to get to that shower."

"You think you're fine, but you won't feel that way when you get to be my age and you're still alone." May smoothed her hands down her thighs. "A woman has needs, you know."

Cassie couldn't believe she was having this conversation. "Mom, I'm okay. Really." More than okay, considering what had just happened in her bedroom. What might happen again if she could get her mother to leave.

"I don't like to think of you spending your life alone. Now, what do you think of trying to get back together with Robert?"

Cassie ground her teeth together. "No. Never."

"All right, dear, if you don't want Robert, I can't make you go back to him. We'll just have to find a man who suits you." She opened her purse and took out a notepad and pen. "Now tell me, what are you looking for in a man?"

Cassie glanced toward the bedroom. "I really don't have time for this discussion now."

"Nonsense. It will only take a moment. Now tell me, what's your idea of the perfect man?"

She sighed knowing she might as well give in against the force of May. She leaned back, considering the question. "I want someone who's a good listener," she said. "Someone who will encourage me and be there for me. Someone who will share his dreams with me."

May made note of all this and looked up expectantly. "What about looks?"

Cassie nodded, thinking of the man in her bedroom now. "Someone good-looking would be nice. But that's not the most important thing."

Her mother smiled knowingly. "That's what you young women all say. Now, what about sex? You want a good sex life, don't you?"

Cassie almost smiled. Sex with Guy certainly wouldn't be a problem.

"I'll take that as a yes." May wrote on her pad. "He needs to be someone who can make a good living. Being poor and in love is all very well for the movies, but in real life, it sucks."

"Mother!"

"Well, it does, dear."

Guy was certainly well-off.... She shook her head. What was she doing? She and Guy had no future together. "Whoever I marry should be someone I have a lot in common with," she said.

Her mother nodded and wrote this down.

"What do you plan to do with this list?" Cassie asked.

May closed the notebook and replaced it in her purse. "This will help us narrow the field."

"Us? Mom, I don't need your help finding a man."

"You certainly haven't done very well on your own, have you?"

Cassie glared at her mother. "If I hear of any classified advertisements placed in my name, I swear I'll never speak to you again."

"Oh, dear, I would never do anything so crass as advertise." May smiled. "I'm merely going to circulate this among my friends and see if they have any eligible sons or nephews or neighbors."

Cassie had a picture of herself as the main topic of conversation at the next Ladies' Luncheon. She sighed. "Mom, you'd really better go."

"All right, dear. Promise me you'll wear something nice tonight. You never know when you might meet an eligible man."

Cassie practically pushed her mother out the door, then returned to the bedroom. Guy was lounging back against the pillows. He grinned when she walked in. "So looks don't matter?" he asked.

"You were eavesdropping."

He sat up, the covers falling dangerously low on his hips. "I've always been a good listener."

She picked up his jeans from the floor and tossed them at him. "I think you'd better get dressed and leave."

"Leave? We were just getting started."

She dropped onto the foot of the bed. "I'm not in the mood anymore."

"I can fix that." He raised up on all fours and crawled toward her.

She pushed him away. "Guy, it's never going to work. The only thing we have in common is good sex."

"Then you admit it's good."

"It's great. But you can't build a relationship on that."

"I'm willing to try."

She turned toward him. "See, it's all about sex with you. I have to have more."

He sat back. "You won't even give me a chance."

"Why put ourselves through this?" She looked away. "Maybe if we'd started off differently..." She shook her head. There was no sense prolonging this agony. "You'd better go now."

She didn't wait for his answer, but went into the bathroom to change. She didn't come out until she heard the front door latch. Had she been wrong to send him away? The problem was, she couldn't think rationally when he was around. Especially when they were both naked.

She picked up the jar of chocolate from the nightstand and stared into it. It would be better this way. Surely it would. She scooped up a fingerful of chocolate and stuck it in her mouth, tears stinging her eyes. It would have tasted better on Guy.

12

"AMY, YOU'VE GOT TO HELP ME."

Amy looked up from a stack of invoices and studied Guy over the top of a pair of black-rimmed glasses. "Why does that statement make me nervous?"

"I'm not joking here. I need a woman's advice and you're the only woman I can ask."

"Mom's a woman, and she's probably more inclined to want to help you than I am." She turned her attention back to the invoices.

He shoved his hands in his pocket, fighting the urge to rip the papers from her hand. "I can't talk to Mom about this. I don't even want to talk to you about it, but I'm desperate."

She took off her glasses and studied him. "You do look a little green around the gills. What happened to get you so upset? And what makes you think I can help?"

"I need you to explain women to me."

"Ah. I should have known this would have something to do with a woman." She set aside the invoices. "What happened?"

He planted his hands on the counter and leaned toward her. "Tell me one thing—why would a woman act like things were great one minute and ask me to leave the next?"

"I don't know. What did she say?"

He frowned. "Before or after she invited me into her bedroom?"

"After. When she asked you to leave."

As if he'd ever forget those words. The rejection still cut deep. "She said it was all about sex for me, and she needed more."

Amy nodded. "And is it?"

"Is it what?"

"Is it all about sex for you?"

"No."

She leaned closer and stared into his eyes. "Remember who you're talking to here. I'm not some potential girlfriend you need to float a load of bull past. Tell the truth—is sex the main issue here, or is there more?"

He took a deep breath. "There's more. A lot more."

Amy's eyes narrowed. "Who is the woman we're talking about here?"

He hesitated, trying to gauge how upset Amy would be about this. But she was going to have to know sooner or later. "It's Cassie."

"Oh." She gathered up the invoices again and straightened the edges. "You don't think you're rushing things a little?"

"I don't know what to think." He gave her a pleading look. "Tell me what to do."

She grew still and raised her eyes to meet him. "I think if you're really serious—and granted, I think you could be making a big mistake—but if you're really serious about Cassie, then you need to change courses."

"What do you mean, 'change courses'? Is that some kind of female code talk?"

"I mean you need to approach her differently than you would someone you only wanted to get into bed."

Guy was skeptical. Then again, Amy *was* a woman, with an insight into another woman's mind that he could never have. "So what should I do differently?"

She propped her elbows on the counter and considered the question. "Tell me about what happened."

"I went over to Cassie's apartment and gave her a little gift and the next thing I know we're all over each other and she invites me into her bedroom." An image of a chocolate-smeared Cassie made him grow hard.

"What happened then?" Amy prompted.

He shrugged. "Her mother came over and Cassie went to get rid of her. Then she came back and told me to get lost and made that 'all about sex' comment."

"What was the gift?" Amy asked.

Guy reddened. "It was, uh, body chocolate."

She giggled. "Body chocolate?"

"Yeah, you know, you paint it on and, uh, lick it off."

"There you have it." She held out her hand.

"Have what?"

"You went over there with a sex-oriented gift. Within five minutes of walking in the door, you're headed for the bedroom. How can she *not* think all you're interested in is sex?"

"She was interested, too."

Amy nodded. "Yes, but then her mother came over and reminded her that a man won't buy a cow when he can get the milk for free."

There she went, talking in female code again. "Her mother didn't say anything about milk."

Amy smiled. "She didn't have to. Simply by virtue of being a mother, she reminded Cassie that nice girls don't sleep around with men who aren't serious about them."

"I told you, I *am* serious about Cassie."

Amy crossed her arms over her chest and gave him a stern look. "Then prove it. Show her you can relate to her on something besides a sexual level. If you can."

"Of course I can." He sagged against the counter. "How am I going to do that if she won't even talk to me?"

Amy shook her head. "That, big brother, is your problem."

SUNDAY MORNING, Cassie was stepping out of the shower when the doorbell rang. What was it with showers and doorbells and telephones? She could sit in front of the television all afternoon and the place would be quiet as the Bear's Thumb at 4:00 a.m. But the minute she dropped her last bit of clothing and turned on the water, bells started ringing. Worse yet, it was seldom anyone she wanted to talk to.

Ding-dong! Ding-dong!

She pulled a towel from the rack and resisted the urge to shout for whoever it was to go away. It was probably a salesman or some fringe evangelist.

Ding-dong!

Sheesh, they were leaning on the bell. Who would be so persistent? And who would be out on a Sunday morning anyway? Then she remembered it was February—Girl Scout cookie season. The image of a little girl in a Brownie uniform filled her head. She wouldn't want to disappoint a little Girl Scout. Besides, she had a sudden craving for a box of Thin Mints.

As the door buzzer continued to sound, she wrapped a towel around her wet hair, pulled on a robe and ran to answer the door.

Her mouth was all set for the flavor of mint and chocolate, only to be quickly replaced by a sour taste. Bob, dressed in jeans and a down coat, leaned against the doorframe. He clutched a bottle of champagne like a club and leered at her. "Hello, kitten," he said, addressing the neckline of her robe. "I see you're ready and waiting for me."

She tried to slam the door, but he blocked the move with his foot. "Bob, go away," she said.

"Go away?" He raised his eyebrows in an expression of mock hurt. "I only just got here, and look, I brought some bubbly." He waggled the bottle at her.

"I don't want your champagne." She didn't want anything from him ever again. "Now please, leave."

He set the bottle on a table just inside the door and turned to her, his expression solemn. "I don't think you'll be asking me to leave when you hear what I have to say."

Her mind raced through the possibilities. He was moving to Alaska? He and Mary Ann were getting married and they wanted her to cater the reception? He'd won the lottery and decided to give her half?

To her astonishment, he dropped to one knee and grasped the hem of her robe. "Cassie, I've decided it's time we got married."

She stared. From this vantage point, she could see the beginnings of a bald spot on the top of his head. In a few years, he'd have a natural tonsure. He'd look like a monk. The thought sent laughter bubbling through her. A giggle escaped.

Bob looked up. "Did you say something?"

She bit her lip and shook her head, unable to speak.

"I understand. This is an important moment in a woman's life. You're too overcome to speak." He stood and seized her, pulling her close and loosening the belt of her robe at the same time.

She responded automatically, raising her knee, catching him right in the crotch.

He hurtled back, doubled over and howling. "Is that any way to treat your future husband?"

"You are not my future husband." She crossed her arms over her chest and glared at him. "I do not intend to marry you now, next month or any time in the next sixty years."

He straightened his coat and scowled. "Why not? We had two good years together. Are you really going to throw all that away?" His expression softened. "Remember those wonderful Sunday afternoons, when you'd make all that great food and the guys would come over to watch the game? Then afterward, you'd give me a back rub and we'd make love on the sofa?" He reached for her. "I miss those Sundays, Cass."

"Of course *you* miss them. You miss having me there to wait on you hand and foot."

"If you didn't like doing it, why did you?"

She winced. Because she'd thought that's what you had to do to keep a man. Put your life on hold and cater to his needs. It was such a painful, outdated thought, it hurt her to admit she'd believed it. "I don't want to wait on anybody anymore," she said. "I want to do what *I* want now."

"I'm sure we could work out some compromise," he said. "Some Sundays we could order in pizza."

"Order your own pizza, Bob."

His surprised look made her want to laugh again. She tightened the belt on her robe. "Now you'd better leave, before I call the police."

He glared at her and took a step back. "You've changed, Cassie, and not for the better. The woman I know and love would never have assaulted me that way."

She rolled her eyes. "The woman you know and love doesn't exist."

"You used to be so sweet." He shook his head. "I don't know what happened to you. I only hope you come to your senses before you've driven away all your friends."

He left, slamming the door behind him. She sank onto the sofa, feeling sick to her stomach. To think she had once imagined she loved him. He was so self-centered, so cheap, so belittling to her. What had she seen in him?

She hugged her arms around her. He was the first man who had ever paid much attention to her. He had made her believe he was the only one who ever would. He'd told her enough times that she was lucky to find a man like him, and she'd believed him.

Until that night at Aspen Creek, when Guy Walters had shown her a different kind of man. A man who in one night treated her with more respect than Bob had shown her in the two years they'd been together.

Bob's last words echoed in her head. *You've changed.* Yes, she'd changed. One weekend of following her heart had convinced her she couldn't live any longer as Conventional Cassie, who never dared to be different. She'd thought dreams were things to be enjoyed only while sleeping, then she'd awakened in Guy's arms, living a dream, and suddenly a whole world of possibilities beckoned.

Had she gone too far? Was she throwing out the good things in her life along with the bad? Would she even recognize her mistakes until it was too late?

She stood and returned to the bathroom. She unwound the towel from her hair and fluffed it with her fingers, then began to dress. She'd planned to stay home and clean house today, but now she couldn't bear to spend another minute here. She needed to be out in the fresh air, involved in some physical activity.

She glanced out the bathroom window, at the clear skies and bright sun. Skiing would be good today. It had been a long time since she'd had her skis out—too long. A day on the slopes would clear away the confusion that almost overwhelmed her, and help her figure out which direction she should steer her life.

Twice each season Mountain Outfitters hosted a display of equipment at Eldora ski resort. The displays brought in business and offered a good excuse to spend a work day in the sun and snow. Sunday morning, Guy and two of his employees, Mike and Jenny, loaded a van with the latest telemark equipment and set up at the base of the Challenge lift. For a small fee, skiers could try out the equipment and, if they decided to buy, receive a discount at the store.

Guy's snowboard was in a rack on top of the van. If business got slow, he hoped to have time to make a couple of runs. So far, though, business at the booth had been brisk. The perfect combination of fresh snow and bright sunshine had brought out skiers and boarders in force. It was the kind of day that spoiled Colorado skiers for any other conditions. The only thing that would make it better would be having someone to share it with.

As Guy helped a petite blonde find the right size boots, he wondered what Cassie was doing this morning. Had she given up skiing, along with her dream of racing, or was she out in the snow this morning? Eldora offered the closest skiing to Boulder—was it too much to hope he'd run into her here? Maybe here on the slopes, away from the bedroom, he'd have a chance to start over with her, to prove she meant more to him than any woman ever had.

About noon, he took a break and went into the lodge to use the restroom. When he came out, he glanced over at the lift line, gauging his chances to make a quick run during the lunchtime lull. A bright pink jacket caught his eye and he smiled, remembering Cassie's jacket, and the way she'd looked that afternoon at Aspen Creek, standing on his doorstep at the condo.

He blinked as the woman shuffled forward on her skis. Were his eyes playing tricks on him, or was that really Cassie? She negotiated a turn in the line so that she was facing him. His heart beat faster. It *was* Cassie.

He took the steps down from the deck two at a time and raced to the booth. His co-workers, Mike and Jenny, were seated in lawn chairs, sharing a sack lunch. "Can you guys handle the booth on your own for a little while?" he asked.

"Sure, boss," Mike said. He grinned. "Going to make a run?"

"Yeah," Guy called over his shoulder, already sprinting toward his van.

By the time he'd collected his board, goggles and gloves and made it back to the lift, Cassie had already gone up. He slid into line, impatiently shifting his weight from one foot to the other as the line moved at a snail's pace.

Finally, it was his turn. He rode up with a pair of skiers from Texas, who raved about the weather and great conditions while Guy listened with only half an ear. He was busy scanning the runs below the lift, searching for a bright pink jacket.

He unloaded from the lift and stepped into his board, then contemplated his choices. If Cassie had once aspired to be a ski racer, she must be fairly competent on the slopes. He discarded the green runs. That left two blue runs and a black. One of the blues ran under the lift and he hadn't seen her on it. Would she take the black, or go for a more relaxing ride on the blue?

He opted for the blue. He started down it, as quickly as he dared without being reckless. The fresh powder whispered under him as he carved turns, plumes of snow arcing behind him as he cut back across the slope. A train of children, led by a ski instructor, glided past him, their laughter drifting back to him on the stiff breeze.

He scanned the expanse of snow spread out below him, watching for a blonde in a pink jacket. Two thirds of the way down, he spotted her. She was resting at the top of a hill, poles planted, gazing out at the valley below.

"Cassie!" he shouted, but the wind swallowed up his voice.

He shoved off and started down, but miscalculated and went shooting past her. When he tried to stop, he overbalanced and fell forward, making a long slide facedown in the snow.

By the time he rolled over and brushed the snow from his face, she'd skied down to him. "Are you all right?" She leaned over him, voice tight with worry.

He raked a handful of snow out of his hair. "I hear having snow shoved up your nose is actually good for your sinuses."

She laughed, a good sign.

He rolled forward, onto his knees. "It's a great way to make an impression on a woman, too."

Her smile faded. "Did you follow me up here?"

He stood and brushed snow from his chest. "Guess I'm beginning to seem like a stalker, huh?" He shook his head. "No, this time I didn't follow you. The store has a display set up at the base of the lift."

"Telemark stuff, right? I remember seeing it—I didn't realize it was you."

"Are you here by yourself?" he asked.

She nodded. "I needed a break, to get away and think."

What are you thinking about so much? he wanted to ask. *Do any of your thoughts have to do with me?* Instead, he stepped back into his bindings. "Want to make a run with me?"

"Sure." She shifted on her skis and was off, carving perfect turns down the steeps, snow arcing out behind her skis. Guy followed, dividing his attention between the terrain and the pink-jacketed figure ahead. She had a natural grace on skis, an agility and confidence he hadn't seen in her before. *She would have been a great racer,* he thought. *Too bad she let other people talk her out of it.*

They slid to a stop at the lift line entrance. He glanced toward the booth, but business was still slow. Mike saw him, grinned at Cassie and gave him a thumbs-up sign.

They rode the lift up together, the silence thick between them. Guy resorted to the banality of strangers. "Beautiful day, isn't it?"

She nodded, but seemed preoccupied.

"I was watching you ski just now," he said. "You're really good."

She shrugged. "I'm a little out of practice."

"Then with practice, you'd be fantastic. I'll bet you could still race if you wanted to."

She looked at him for the first time since he'd fallen in front of her. The amber lenses of her goggles made it hard to read her expression, but he thought she seemed interested. "You think so? I figured I was past that."

"No way. You ought to give it a try. Aspen Creek is

holding its Winter Carnival Downhill in a couple of weeks."

"You really think I should enter?"

He patted her hand, wishing they weren't both wearing thick gloves. More than anything, he wanted to touch her. "What have you got to lose?"

She didn't say anything else. When they got off the lift, she took off ahead of him, forcing him once again to follow her lead.

They made the run without stopping, without talking. The elation Guy had felt when he'd first seen her faded with each cut of his board into the powdery snow. He'd hoped for an afternoon spent getting to know each other better. Instead, she wasn't even talking to him. Was she still angry over last night's visit to her apartment? Had he gone too far with his praise of her ability? Did she think he wasn't sincere?

Maybe he'd best give up while he was ahead. Cassie obviously wasn't interested in having anything to do with him today. At the lift line again, he stepped out of his bindings. "I'd better get back to work."

To his surprise, she took off her skis and followed him toward the booth. "I need a break anyway," she said by way of explanation.

He introduced her to Mike and Jenny, then checked the clipboard listing equipment checkouts. "So how's business?" he asked.

"Slow." Mike glanced at Jenny, who nodded in agreement. "In fact, we've been talking and Jenny and I think we can handle things. You ought to take the afternoon off and enjoy yourself."

Guy looked at Cassie. "What do you think? You said

you came up here to sort things out. If you want to be alone, that's okay with me."

She ran her hand along the edge of the counter. "That's okay. I...why don't we spend the afternoon together?"

He couldn't hold back a smile, which turned into a grin when she smiled back at him. With hasty good-byes to Mike and Jenny, they hurried to reclaim her skis and his board. "Let's try some of the runs off the Indian Peaks lift," she suggested.

Though their conversation was limited, the mood between them had lightened. He challenged her to a race to the bottom, which he won by mere inches. She pulled up beside him, turning at the last minute to spray snow over him, laughing as he threw up his hands to fend off the snow shower. "How about grabbing a bite at the grill?" he asked.

"That sounds good."

Over burgers and fries on the outdoor deck, Cassie apologized for her earlier silence. "I guess I've been a little preoccupied," she said. "I'm sorry."

"That's okay," Guy said. "I'm the one who intruded on your day."

She swirled a French fry in a pool of ketchup. "Bob came by to see me this morning."

Mustard oozed out of his burger as he squeezed it a little too hard. He struggled to keep his voice even. "You want me to talk to him? Tell him to stop hassling you?"

She shook her head. "I don't think he'll be back."

He sipped from a can of pop, waiting for what would come next. Had she told the jerk off for good?

"He asked me to marry him."

Pop stung his nose as he choked back a gasp. "He what?"

"He asked me to marry him." She bit the end off a fry and chewed, a thoughtful expression on her face. "To think of all those months when I waited and waited for him to pop the question, and he does it now."

He tightened the grip on the soda can. "What did you say?"

She gave him a teasing look. "What do you think I said?"

"I hope you told him he was crazy to think you'd ever marry him."

She laughed. "That's about the size of it."

He relaxed his grip and sat back in his chair. "How did he take it?"

She pushed aside the rest of her hamburger, all trace of a smile vanished. "He told me I'd changed. That I was going to drive away all my friends."

He leaned forward and put his hand over hers. "You won't drive me away."

"Thanks. Still, it hurt to hear that."

"Some people don't like change. It's hard for them to handle."

She nodded. "It's hard for me, too."

He stroked her hand, so soft. He took it in his and began massaging the fingers. He wanted to touch so much more, but he sensed he needed to take it slow. "You know what I see when I look at you?"

She met his gaze. "What do you see?"

"I see a young woman who's only beginning to dis-cover what she could be. Someone who's kept the best part of herself hidden, until now." He kissed her palm. "You remember that night in Aspen Creek?"

She laughed, sounding out of breath. "As if I'd ever forget."

"That night we spent together, the biggest turn-on for me was the fact that you were so seductive, and yet so innocent. You're such a mixture of prim and passionate."

She leaned toward him, eyes dark with desire, lips slightly parted. He reached for her, ready to gather her into his arms, to kiss her to the edge of control.

"Guy! Hey, Guy!"

They jerked apart as a slender man with a blond ponytail jogged up to their table. "Hello, Dave." Guy stifled a groan.

Dave looked from Guy to Cassie and grinned. "Not the best timing, huh?"

"Dave, this is Cassie Carmichael. Cassie, my buddy in the Boulder Bandidos, Dave Reese."

Cassie and Dave shook hands. "You're the man who's getting married soon," she said.

Dave's smile broadened. "That's me." He clapped Guy on the shoulder. "I wanted to tell you to save Saturday after next on your calendar, man. Susan's friends are throwing us a couple shower and I expect to see you there."

"A shower?" Guy made a face. "Isn't that for the bride-to-be and her girlfriends?"

"Not anymore, dude. Now they throw these couple showers. Instead of her and the bridesmaids oohing and aahing over blenders and bath towels, I get to help open power tools and bar sets. So you'll be there, okay?" He turned to Cassie. "You, too. It'll be a fun party."

Guy shook his head. "You're really getting into this, aren't you?" he said.

Dave laughed. "You should try it some time." He took a couple of steps back and waved. "I gotta go now. Susan's waiting in the lift line. I cut out to say hi to you guys." He nodded to Cassie. "Nice to meet you."

"He seems like a nice guy," Cassie said when he was gone.

"Yeah. And pretty excited about getting married." He watched Dave kiss a pretty brunette on the cheek as he joined her in the lift line below. "Hard to believe I'm the last of the Bandidos to tie the knot." *Maybe my turn is coming,* he thought, his gaze returning to Cassie.

Cassie looked away. "Guy, I want you to know I like you...a lot." She laced her fingers together and rested them in her lap. "But I need time to figure out what I want in life, where I'm going. I...I'm not ready to jump back into a relationship." She glanced up at him, her eyes questioning.

"In other words, you want to be 'just friends.'" He tried not to let his disappointment show, but to his own ears, his voice sounded tense.

"I guess that is what I'm saying. Is it too much to ask?"

From any other woman, yes. He wanted more from Cassie than mere friendship—much more. He wasn't ready to give up on her yet. He nodded. "I can wait."

Though he intended to do everything in his power to make that wait as short as possible.

"Then I have a favor to ask."

"Ask."

"You coached your sister, Amy, when she was on the college ski team, didn't you?"

He nodded.

"Do you think you could coach me? For the Aspen Creek race?"

He leaned closer, trying to read her expression. "You're going to go for it, then?"

She looked him in the eye. "I'm going to go for it. I think I'm ready to take a few more risks in my life."

Guy's heart pounded as if he'd just run up Long's Peak. Cassie's words had asked for his help, but the emotion in her eyes told him if he bided his time she could very well end up asking for his heart.

13

MONDAY MORNING, Cassie was still in her bathrobe, slugging down her first cup of coffee of the day, when her doorbell rang. She groaned. Surely no Girl Scouts were out this early in the morning, and none of her friends got out of bed before nine if they could possibly avoid it. That left only one likely culprit.

Ding-dong!

"Go away!" she shouted. Bob obviously hadn't gotten the message yesterday, if he'd returned this morning for another try.

Bam-bam-bam!

Great! He was pounding on the door now. Next thing she knew, grumpy Mr. Fitz next door would be calling the police. She shoved back her chair and headed for the door, snatching up one of her ski poles as she passed the pile of equipment she'd dumped by the sofa. If Bob didn't understand plain English, maybe physical threats would make an impression. One thing for certain, he wasn't setting foot in her apartment again.

Bam-bam-bam!

As the pounding continued, she stood on tiptoe and peered through the peephole. *Just wait till I finish giving that man a piece of my mind....*

She yelped and jumped back as she looked into a pair of sapphire eyes. Eyes that sent a lightning bolt of heat through her. Eyes that made her think of tangled sheets, naked flesh and the kind of lovemaking that required not just a bedroom, but the whole damned honeymoon suite.

She tucked the ski pole under one arm and fumbled for the lock, finally succeeding in jerking open the door.

Guy stood on the threshold, grinning. "Good morning," he said.

"Guy, what are you doing here?"

"I came to take you running." He stepped into the apartment and nodded toward the ski pole. "What's with the weapon?"

She leaned the pole against the back of the sofa, trying to regain some of her composure. "I was expecting Bob." Instead, she'd found the one man she might have nominated as "most likely to talk her out of her clothes." She cinched her robe tighter.

"I wouldn't risk ruining a good pole for the likes of him." Guy rubbed his hands together. "Next time, try a rolling pin."

"There won't be a next time." She retrieved her coffee from the table and took a long sip. Cooler, but she welcomed caffeine in any form.

He came up behind her, so close the edge of his fleece jacket brushed against her robe. When he spoke, his breath tickled the back of her neck. "Are you ready to run?"

Why bother? she thought. *My heart's already racing.*

She looked down at her bathrobe. "Oh, sure. I always dress like this for any kind of athletic activity."

He raised one eyebrow. "I can think of at least one activity that would be appropriate for."

Was it possible for a person's entire body to blush? She crossed her arms over her chest and moved away from him. "Why are you here, Guy? It's six-thirty in the morning. I have to get ready for work."

"You've got plenty of time. I'm your coach, remember, and coach says we have to get those legs in shape for racing." His gaze dropped to her bare calves. "Though I must say, I do like the shape they're in already."

She glanced out the window. "It must be fifteen degrees out there."

"Nice and crisp. Just the thing to wake you up." He made a shooing motion with his hand. "Go on, get dressed. And remember to wear layers."

She escaped into the bedroom and blindly began pulling clothes out of drawers. As she donned stretch pants, sports bra and fleece pullover, she was aware of Guy moving around in the other room. She couldn't help remembering their last encounter here, when she had undressed for him.

"I must have been crazy to ask him to coach me," she muttered as she gathered her hair into a ponytail. "I want us to be just *friends*," she mimicked. "I might as well wish Everest was just another mountain."

She slathered sunscreen across her nose. No two ways about it, she wanted Guy. Spending time with him was a bad idea.

"Who are you talking to in there?" Guy called through the door.

"No one." She grabbed up a parka and dashed into the living room.

She grumbled through warm-up stretches and refused to say anything at all for the first three blocks of their run. But as her muscles loosened and the rest of her came awake, she began to appreciate the unusual sensation of being out and about when most people were just getting started with their day. The chilled air rushed into her lungs, carrying the scent of pine. Sunrise painted the mountains in seashell shades of pink and orange.

"Tell the truth, you're glad you came now, aren't you?"

She glanced at Guy. He ran with easy grace, legs stretching out in long strides, feet hitting the pavement in a steady rhythm. "Yeah, I'm glad," she admitted. "It's been a long time since I went for a run."

"Why is that?" he asked.

She shrugged. "I guess because I don't like to go alone."

"Then you can come with me. What are friends for?"

She nodded, conversation impossible as they turned onto Broadway and started the push up University Hill. His last words rang in her ears. Friends. Guy seemed to be taking her "friends only" restriction pretty well. Maybe too well. If he really liked her, wouldn't he pursue her more? Wouldn't he try harder to win her?

At the top of the hill, they paused at a park bench to catch their breath. Guy sagged onto the bench and unzipped his jacket. Panting, she eased down beside him. "This...is...disgusting," she gasped. "You're not even... winded."

"I've been trail running for a while now." He glanced at her. "Running in the mountains will get you in shape in no time."

"Trail running." Not her idea of fun. One more example of how the two of them had nothing in common. She unzipped her own jacket. "What made you decide to do that? A sudden urge to torture yourself?"

"Dave got me started. You know, the guy you met yesterday."

She nodded. "The one who's getting married."

"That's the one. Did I tell you he asked me to be his best man?"

"Congratulations. That's quite an honor. Are you nervous?"

He shook his head. "Nah. This is the fifth time I've stood up with a buddy at his wedding. All I have to do is keep track of the ring, make a toast at the reception and see to it that the preacher gets paid. At least Dave is getting married at a church. The last wedding I was in, the bride and groom said their vows in a plane, then parachuted into married life."

"You're joking."

His face was serious. "I'm not. I was in another wedding where the bride and groom decided to get married at Loveland Ski Area on Valentine's Day. Most of the wedding party was on skis. We were the twenty-seventh wedding of the day."

She giggled. "Don't you know anyone who has a normal wedding, besides Dave?"

"I've been in two weddings on top of Lookout Mountain. That was pretty normal."

"Except for the spectacular views." She leaned forward, chin in her hands. "What a great place for a wedding." Like any woman, she'd fantasized about what her own wedding would be like. Her dreams had been ordinary ones, of white lace and flowers in the Presbyterian church her mother had attended off and on over the years. Now she wondered if something a little more exciting might appeal to her. Parachuting seemed a little drastic, but a mountaintop ceremony might be just the thing.

"I guess it doesn't really matter where you get married, as long as you're marrying the right person."

She turned and found Guy's gaze on her, his expression unreadable. A warmth spread through her that had nothing to do with the layers of clothing she wore. "I...I think we'd better get going," she stammered. Before he could say anything, she jumped up and started running down the street. *Coward* she thought as she gained speed down the hill. But better to run away from Guy now than to risk losing herself in a another doomed romance.

SLOW DOWN, Guy told himself, but the admonishment had nothing to do with speed. It didn't take a genius to know he'd scared Cassie off with his talk about marriage. He hadn't even intended to say anything—the words had just popped out.

Did that mean he was in love with her? He glanced over at her. She'd slowed her pace some, and her breathing had grown labored, but she was still determined to keep up. She tackled life the same way, gritting her teeth through the bad parts, meeting difficulty head-on. Where he went looking for adventure, Cassie handled whatever came her way as if it were an adventure. She had a good sense of humor, and a passion for everything she did that was contagious. How could he not love a woman like that? The realization stunned him. He couldn't keep from smiling as a tremendous happiness filled him.

I'm in love with Cassie Carmichael. The words sounded in his head in time to his feet hitting the pavement—*I love Cassie. I love Cassie.*

He reached out and took her arm and pulled her to a stop. It took everything he had not to hold her close and kiss her senseless. As it was, she probably thought he'd lost it, he had such an idiotic grin on his face. "Let's wrap it up and grab a bagel somewhere, okay?"

She shook her head, and took a step back from him. "No. I have to go get ready for work."

"Aww, c'mon. You won't be late."

She shook her head. "No. I really have to go."

She turned toward her apartment and he followed. He waited until they'd reached her building before he tried again. She started up the steps, but he put out a hand to stop her. "Have dinner with me tonight."

She shook her head. "I don't think that would be a good idea."

"Not a date." He smiled in a way he hoped wasn't threatening. "Merely part of my duties as your coach to make sure you eat right."

Her lips curved. "Sounds like a pretty flimsy excuse to me."

"Say yes, Cassie. You don't want to sit home alone tonight and brood. Come with me and forget all about what's his name."

This time she laughed. "All right. But Dutch treat. And no place romantic."

"It's a deal. No romance. Not until you're ready."

She tilted her head and studied him. "You're still holding out hope then?"

"Call me an optimist."

She shook her head. "It's only dinner, Guy."

"I know. Just dinner. I'll pick you up at six-thirty."

They said goodbye and he headed for his own place, whistling under his breath. For a man who wasn't getting to first base with the woman he loved, he felt incredibly happy. Maybe falling in love meant losing your mind, a little bit at a time. Ah, but what a way to go.

14

"NOW LET ME GET THIS STRAIGHT." Jill pointed a coffee spoon at Cassie like a weapon. "You're not dating the man. You say you don't want a relationship with anyone right now, but he's taking you to dinner tonight?"

Cassie snatched the spoon out of Jill's hand and dropped it into the silverware basket of the dishwasher. The morning crowd had dispersed, and the two friends were cleaning up. "He's not taking me to dinner. We're only going out to eat."

Jill handed Cassie a stack of coffee mugs. "As if there's a difference. What exactly is going on with you two?"

Cassie hunched her shoulders and pretended to be fascinated with arranging the dirty cups in the dishwasher rack. "Nothing's going on."

"Then why not?" Jill leaned back against the counter and studied her friend. "I don't get it. You spend a fantastic night with the man, he's obviously crazy about you and now you're acting like some Frigid Frieda afraid to even kiss him good-night."

Ouch! When Jill put it that way, Cassie did sound nuts. She shut the dishwasher door and secured the latch. "Maybe that's the problem. We went at this backward."

Jill shrugged. "Maybe you did, but I thought you were through with being timid and conventional. What happened to the wild woman?"

"I guess she went too far into unfamiliar territory." She turned the control dial to start the dishwasher.

Jill leaned closer. "There's something else, isn't there? Come on, you can tell me."

"You should consider a job with the FBI. You'd have people confessing their darkest secrets left and right."

Jill folded her arms over her chest. "I'm only trying to help."

Cassie nodded. "I know. But I don't know what to tell you."

"You're not still thinking about quitting Java Jive and leaving me to face the caffeine addicts by myself, are you?"

She made a face. "After you threatened to post my grade school pictures—the ones before I got braces and contacts—on the Net, I decided against it."

"Smart woman. Besides, you need this job to keep you in touch with the public, including Guy."

Cassie stared down at the empty sink. "I'm so confused."

"About what?"

"About everything." She dried her hands on a dishtowel. "Bob came by the apartment yesterday morning and asked me to marry him."

"The man always did have a lousy sense of timing." Jill fished a chocolate biscotti from the jar on the counter and offered half to Cassie. "I hope you told him to take a hike."

"I did, more or less." Cassie nibbled the biscotti.

"But his visit reminded me of what a doormat I was around him. It was like I was brainwashed, or something."

"Maybe you were, a little bit. I mean, a lot of women start out doing things for a man because they really want to make him happy. But they end up thinking they have to keep doing those things so he'll stay happy."

Cassie nodded. "I've learned my lesson. From now on, I think about what makes me happy first. No more doing things I don't like just to please some man."

"Guy doesn't want you to do things you don't like, does he?"

Guy again. Everything always came back to him, didn't it? She moved away from Jill, down the counter, where she absently began making a fresh pot of coffee. "Yeah, well, he still thinks I'm the wild woman he met at Aspen Creek."

"I don't think you give the man enough credit. I think he wants you for who you are—the wild woman and the good girl."

Did he? The wild woman was the one who had made love to him in Aspen Creek. And in the bedroom at her apartment. She was the one he'd convinced to enter the ski race. What did he really know about Cassie's more conventional side?

The phone rang and Cassie answered it. "Java Jive, where the coffee—"

"I'm not a customer, you don't have to sell me anything."

Cassie sighed. "Hello, Mom. What's up?" *Please don't let Bob have called again.*

"Did you know that Susan Michaels is getting married?"

"Who is Susan Michaels?" *And what does this have to do with me?*

"You remember Susan, don't you? The nice girl who lived down the street when we had the house in Nederland."

"Mom, I was ten years old."

"Well, her parents have kept in touch and they told me the good news."

"Good for her."

"See, other women your age agree with me that marriage is a good thing. We just have to find the right man for you."

Cassie stifled a groan. "Mom, don't start again."

"I'm only thinking of you, dear. Some of the happiest years of my life have been as a new bride."

You certainly have a lot of experience there. But Cassie held her tongue. "I appreciate your concern, Mom, but I'm all right. Really."

"I'm not saying you have to run off with the first man you see, but it won't hurt you to get out more, meet more men."

Cassie shook her head. The men she already knew were trouble enough. She certainly didn't need to meet more of them. "I've taken up ski racing again, Mom. I've entered the Aspen Creek Downhill next month."

"Oh, dear. Do you think you should? Aren't you worried you'll get big thigh muscles? Not at all attractive, dear. If you want a winter sport, why not ice skating? It's so graceful, and you could wear those cute short skirts. So sexy."

"I like ski racing, Mom. I'm doing it for me, not to meet men."

"If you keep thinking like that, you'll end up lonely and alone." She sniffed. "And I'll never have grandchildren."

"You should think about getting a dog, Mom. A nice poodle or something. I have to go now."

She hung up, and slumped back down on the stool. "You should have told her about Guy," Jill said. "One look at him and she'd forget all about Bob."

Cassie shook her head. "No, things are too uncertain between us."

"Come on. The man's in love with you."

"Or maybe he only loves his *idea* of me." She shook her head. "I wish I could be sure."

"You can't." Jill drained her cup and set it in the sink. "That's why falling in love is such a thrill. There's that element of risk."

"I've never been much for risk."

Jill laughed. "That's the old Cassie talking, for sure. You don't call racing down a mountain on two fiberglass slats risky? Or talking your way into a handsome man's bedroom so you could seduce him? You're a lot more daring than you give yourself credit for."

"Maybe you're right." But was she willing to risk loving Guy, knowing they both might end up disappointed?

GUY KNEW he was in trouble when Cassie met him at the door dressed in an old University of Colorado sweatshirt. "Did you forget we're going to dinner?" he asked after she'd invited him inside.

"I didn't forget." She grabbed her purse from the kitchen counter and turned to him. "I'm all ready to go, coach."

Coach. So she was still determined to keep him at a distance. As if an old sweatshirt would do that. "I thought we might go to Colacci's," he said. He took out his car keys. "Pasta's always a good training meal and they have some of the best homemade ravioli."

"I've got a better idea. There's a new place I've been dying to try."

Twenty minutes later, they were seated in a booth in the White Rabbit restaurant, surrounded by pots of flowers. Sitar music twanged in the background, and the only light came from an astonishing collection of lava lamps. Guy squinted at the handwritten menu. Tofu tandoori. Bean and basmati bake. Sprout surprise.

He flipped to the back and read listings for wheat grass juice, alfalfa shakes and spirulina shots. He laid the menu aside and his stomach growled.

"Is something wrong?" Cassie looked up at him.

"I can't find any meat on this menu."

She laughed. "Of course not. This is a vegetarian restaurant."

"I've heard of those, but I've never actually been in one."

"I've heard the food here is great." Why was she smirking at him that way?

Cassie ordered some kind of salad. Guy ordered a vegetarian burger, reasoning that at least it looked like meat. "I got a look at the entry list for the Aspen Creek Downhill today," he said when the waitress left them alone again.

"Oh?" She stirred sugar into her hibiscus tea. "How'd you manage that?"

"Our store is one of the sponsors. There are some pretty big names on there. I recognized Tammy Simmons. She was a teammate of yours and Amy's."

She added lemon to her tea. "I remember her. She's really good."

"You're good, too."

"How do you know? You haven't seen me race in years."

He grinned. "But you've got a great coach."

The arrival of the waiter with their food cut off her answer. They avoided each other's gazes, busying themselves dressing salad and burger. After a long while, Cassie let out a sigh.

He looked up at her. "What is it?"

She poked at her sprout salad, apparently looking for something in there that was edible. "Maybe I'm in over my head. Maybe I should start smaller."

"No, no, I think you have a great chance."

"A great chance to make a fool of myself."

"Is that what you're afraid of?"

"I seem to have a knack for it, don't you think?"

He shoved aside his half-eaten burger and reached across the table for her hand. "What are you talking about?"

She tried to pull away from his grasp, but he held her fast. "That's what I did with you in Aspen Creek, isn't it? Made a fool of myself?"

"I didn't see it that way at all. I didn't think you did, either. What makes you think so now?"

Her gaze met his, not beaten, as he'd expected, but

defiant. "I know you think I'm some kind of female daredevil, but I'm really a very ordinary person."

"You say that, but I don't see anything ordinary about you." He stroked her hand, tracing the contours of her palm with his thumb. "What happened at Aspen Creek was pretty extraordinary. And the other day in your apartment was even more so."

She succeeded in pulling her hand away this time. "That's not really me. At least not all of me. One of these days you'll find that out."

"And I'll be disappointed—is that what you think?"

She looked away, silent. The answer was there in her lowered eyes and in the downward curve of her mouth.

He slid from the booth and pulled two twenties from his wallet and left them on the table. "Come on. Let's get out of here."

I'VE DONE IT NOW, Cassie thought as she followed Guy out of the restaurant. *I've made him mad and now he's taking me home.* Polite as always, he opened the car door for her and she slid in, keeping as far to the passenger side as possible and avoiding looking at him.

She told herself she ought to be happy she'd finally gotten through to him that they weren't right for each other, but instead she felt sick and sad.

They stopped at the light on Canyon and she waited for him to turn left to head back up to her apartment. But when the light changed, he kept straight on Twenty-eighth. She sat up straighter. "Where are you going?"

"Someplace I promised to take you a while back." He glanced at her, his expression revealing nothing.

Curious, she settled back in the seat and stared out the window at the busy city streets. But when the car began the climb up Flagstaff Road, she tensed. "Guy, you can't be serious!"

"Why not? I promised you dinner at the Flagstaff House once. The least we can do is have dessert there after all that rabbit food I just endured."

"But we're not dressed for a place like that." She looked down at her sweatshirt. The Flagstaff House was a high heels and suit and tie kind of place.

"Don't worry. The mâitre d' is a friend of mine. He'll slip us in."

She hugged her arms across her chest and frowned at him. "You agreed—no place fancy."

He grinned. "I changed my mind."

While they waited in the valet parking line behind two stretch limos, Cassie alternated between anger and panic. What did Guy think he was doing, bringing her to such a blatantly romantic place? Did he think he could soften her resolve to keep their relationship on a platonic level? Did he think a spectacular view and heavenly chocolate mousse would distract her from her goals?

Panic took over when she acknowledged the possibility that he might succeed. She was as susceptible to romance as the next girl, and considering the man doing the romancing was also the sexiest man she'd ever met... There were plenty of people who'd say she ought to have her head examined for putting him off. Sometimes she wondered if they weren't right.

It would be so easy to give in. To go with the flow of a relationship with Guy and see where it would lead. But she'd tried that approach to life before and it hadn't gotten her anywhere good. No. Better to train for the Aspen Creek downhill, finish her schooling and get her life in order before she tackled another relationship.

The doorman opened the passenger-side door and offered his hand, but the smile vanished from his face when he took in Cassie's casual clothes. Guy tossed his keys to the valet and took Cassie's hand from the doorman. "Is Jack here tonight?" he asked.

Mute, the doorman nodded. Guy thanked him and led Cassie toward the door. She kept her head down, watching out of the corner of her eye as women in evening gowns and men in suits or even tuxedos milled around in the foyer, collecting coats or waiting for the valets to deliver cars.

Guy slipped his arm around her. "Hey, it's okay. *I* think you look fine."

After a whispered exchange with the maître d', during which Cassie suspected a few bills exchanged hands, they were escorted to a discreet corner table against the glass that made up one wall of the restaurant.

Cassie stared at the lights of Boulder spread out far below her. She tried to find words to describe the scene—thoughts of diamonds and glitter seemed cliched.

"It reminds me of a Lite-Brite set I had as a kid," Guy said.

She laughed. "It does, doesn't it?" She leaned toward the window. "Is that Highway 36 there?" She pointed to a steady string of moving lights.

"Yes, and that glow in the distance is Fort Collins."

"Good evening, and welcome to Flagstaff House." A black-suited waiter appeared at tableside. "May I tell you about our specials this evening?"

"We're here for dessert," Guy said. "And coffee?" He looked at Cassie.

She nodded. The waiter handed her a gold-tasseled dessert menu. A quick scan and she found what she was looking for. "I know what I want. The chocolate mousse."

"Very good. And for you, sir?"

Guy ordered crème brûlée. When the waiter left them, he turned to Cassie. "Now aren't you glad we came here?"

She unrolled her napkin and carefully arranged her silverware in front of her. "I still think you should have kept our bargain."

He sat back and looked out the window. "This is one of my favorite places. I wanted to share it with you."

"Do you come here often?" Her throat tightened on the words. How many other women had Guy brought here?

"It's sort of a family tradition to come here for special occasions—birthdays and my parents' anniversary every year."

Cassie remembered an attractive couple who had attended races with Amy. "How long have your parents been married?"

"Thirty-two years." He shook his head. "Pretty amazing."

"Yes, it is." The waiter arrived with their coffee. Cassie took a sip, and studied Guy over the rim of the fine china cup. He seemed so relaxed. So content with himself, and easy to be with. Had his years of adventuring given him that kind of confidence, or had he come by it naturally?

"What's even more amazing, they've lived in the same house the whole time."

Cassie searched her memory. "A log cabin, right? In Indian Hills?"

"That's right. I'd forgotten you'd been there, with Amy."

She looked down at the table, the guilt she always felt at the mention of her former friend flooding her. "How is she doing? I mean, with her knees and all?"

"She's doing okay. They bother her sometimes, but not too much."

"I guess she's had lots of physical therapy."

"Not for years, but at first she went all the time."

"Could she still ski again, if she wanted?"

"I think so. I'm hoping seeing you racing again will convince her to give it a try."

"Why would you think that?"

"She always admired you. I think that's why she was so disappointed when you left the team."

This revelation left her shaky. "I...I always admired her. When she got hurt, I think I just freaked out." She picked up a spoon and turned it over and over, the polished silver reflecting the candlelight. "I guess you could say Amy inspired me to want to be a massage therapist."

"Oh?" Guy pushed aside his coffee cup. "How's that?"

She laid aside the spoon and looked, not at Guy, but at his reflection in the glass. "I felt so helpless when she was hurt. You know, I had made a run right before her and I saw the accident happen. I'll never forget seeing her lying there in the snow, and hearing her scream." She shook her head, forcing back the horror. "I really wished there was something I could do. Then I attended a health fair and a massage therapist there talked about all the ways massage is used in sports medicine. I knew I couldn't help Amy anymore, but I could help people like her."

Guy reached across the table and took her hand. "I think it would mean a lot to her to know that. It means a lot to me."

The waiter delivered their desserts, forcing them to separate. Cassie focused on regaining the composure she'd come close to losing just then. Why had she told Guy that story? Why now? She was supposed to be keeping her distance with him, not baring her soul.

She dug her spoon into the velvet-smooth mousse, her mouth watering at the thought of the first decadent taste. But the scent of chocolate sharpened another appetite, calling to mind a naked Guy licking chocolate from her breast. She shifted in her seat, fighting desire.

"Is something wrong?" Guy asked.

"No. It's delicious." She gulped the spoonful of mousse, the intense chocolate flavor only increasing her arousal.

"Let me try." He reached across and dug his own spoon into the dish. A smile spread across his lips as he tasted the chocolate. "Almost as good as the last I had."

Cassie blushed, knowing he wasn't talking about mousse. She searched for some neutral change of subject. "So I imagine work keeps you pretty busy these days. Do you have much time for climbing and hang gliding and all those things you used to do?"

"I climb and hike on weekends. I took a ten-day pack trip to Yellowstone in November with my mom and dad." He shrugged. "I guess I don't do as much as when I was younger, but I've got other things I'm interested in now."

She could feel his gaze on her, but refused to meet his eyes. She concentrated on finishing dessert and kept her voice light. "The trip with your mom and dad must have been fun. I envy you. What family I have is scattered all over the place."

He shook his head. "So many people I know grew up in dysfunctional families, I feel like an oddball sometimes, having had it so good."

She laughed. "My mother was married three times. Working on her fourth."

"That must have been tough for you."

There he went, getting serious again. She tried to think of some nonchalant answer, but what came out was more honest. "We moved about six times when I was a kid. I had two different stepfathers. I felt close to them while they were there, but when Mom divorced them, I never saw them again."

"What about your father?"

She pushed away her empty dessert dish. "He wasn't around much." Maybe that was why she had been willing to do almost anything to hang on to any man who came into her life. Who was to say she wouldn't do the same with Guy? Especially with Guy, who made her feel things no man ever had.

"When I marry, I want it to be for life," he said.

The words startled her. She looked up at him, heart in her throat.

He met her gaze, his eyes gentle. "Call me old-fashioned, but I want a marriage like my parents have. A family like the one we had. All that adventure stuff—it's fun and I've had a good time, but family, that's what it's really all about."

The words made her light-headed. What was he saying? That he wanted to have that kind of life with *her?* "Oh, Guy—"

"Shhh. Don't say anything." He reached out and covered her fingers with his own. "Just think about it. Okay?"

She withdrew her hand and looked away from him, toward the Disneyland brightness below. Was it possible to have the kind of happiness Guy talked about in the kind of world they lived in today? He obviously believed it. Could she come to believe it, too? On the other hand, how could she afford not to?

15

"WHY DON'T YOU MAKE another run, but this time, try to go into a tighter tuck, and keep your arms really close to your body." Cassie nodded and headed toward the rope tow that would take her up to the top of the slalom course. Guy watched her, resisting the urge to call her back. *Forget about training,* he wanted to say. *What about us?*

She hadn't said anything at all about her feelings for him, or lack of them, in the week since they'd had dinner together. He'd hoped talking to her about his family and what he wanted in a relationship would change her opinion of him. She had this image of him as some sort of daredevil wild man. Yes, he'd done some pretty crazy things in his life, especially in those high school and college years as one of the Boulder Bandidos. He'd climbed mountains and rafted wild rivers and founded a million-dollar business before he was thirty. But that was only the outer trappings. Inside, he was a perfectly ordinary man who wanted ordinary things—a home, a family, a woman to love.

Not just any woman. He wanted Cassie. She reached the top of the course and signaled that she was ready. He held an orange flag high in one hand and a stopwatch in the other, clicking the watch as he let the flag fall.

Her form was better this time, near perfect even. He leaned forward, knees bent, silently following her progress down the slope. He leaned into the curves as she did, and tucked his elbows in silent imitation, straightening only as she approached the finish line. He clicked the watch as she sped past.

"You shaved off four-tenths of a second this time," he called as she released her bindings.

She shook her head. "Not good enough. I checked and last year even the junior-division winner was faster."

He opened his logbook and recorded the time. "You need better equipment. Real racing gear."

"I can't afford better equipment. Maybe if my skis were tuned differently...."

He shouldered his backpack while she collected her skis and poles. "You need new gear. Your competition will have the best."

"I already told you, I can't afford it."

"You don't have to. I've got a store full of the stuff." He started walking back toward his Jeep.

She hurried to keep up with him, her boots crunching in the snow. "I can't let you do that."

"Why not? Stores sponsor athletes all the time." He paused and looked back at her, admiring the way her racing leotard clung to her shape. "You'd look good with Mountain Outfitters stenciled down each leg."

She made a face. "If your name was any longer, I'd have to be taller."

"If the name was shorter, we could plaster it across your butt."

He started toward the car once more and she fell into step beside him. "Do you really think new equipment will make that much difference?"

He nodded. "I really think it will."

"Then I guess we'd better do it."

They reached the car and he helped her fit her skis in the rack. "You really want to win this, don't you?" he asked.

She grabbed a fleece vest from the front seat and put it on. "Yeah. I really do."

She started to get into the car, but he put a hand on her shoulder and turned her toward him. "Why?" He wanted to know what drove her. Why had she decided to do this now? Did he have anything to do with her decision?

She compressed her lips into a thin line and her eyes darted to the side, as if searching for the right words. "I think...I want to prove to myself that I can follow through with this. It's not even about winning anymore, though I'd like to win. It's more about not giving up on a dream I had once." As she spoke, she became more impassioned, gesturing with her hands, her eyes alight. "I let other people talk me out of racing before. I let them tell me how to live my life. And I don't want to do it again. So I'm entering this race, even if I'm too old and too out of practice."

She leaned forward, peering into his eyes. "Can you understand that, even a little?"

He nodded. "I can." Not because he'd been through anything similar. He hadn't. All his life, when he'd wanted something, he'd gone for it, other people's opinions be damned. When he looked into Cassie's eyes, he sensed a connection. Even though he'd never been through what she was going through, he imagined he could feel what she was feeling.

And he saw the same longing in her that he'd felt, a longing to be complete, to find what was missing in her life. She thought it was being able to hold on to her dreams. He knew the missing link for him was her.

CASSIE THOUGHT of Mountain Outfitters as a big boys'—and girls'—toy store. Every kind of outdoor gear and gadget filled the cavernous stone-and-glass building. Guy led her past a battalion of gleaming bicycles, stacks of crayon-colored kayaks, a mini village of tents and enough boots and backpacks to outfit every hiker in the state. The scent of new leather and nylon perfumed the air and all around her, customers and clerks talked of global positioning systems, Topo! maps, Gore-Tex linings and aluminum frames.

Guy strode through it all like a prince in his kingdom. "Hi, Guy." "Whassup, Guy?" "How you doing, Guy?" greeted him at every turn.

He stopped to shake hands with a clerk in the bicycle department. "Gary, good to see you, man."

He paused in the map section to talk to a customer. "Chris, I see you're finally buying that new GPS system I recommended."

A wall of red rock rose up in the middle of the building. "What is that?" Cassie stopped to stare at the array of ropes and cables swinging from the rock.

"It's a climbing wall. Latest thing in outdoor stores."

They moved on, and another customer hailed him in the boot department. "Carol, let me know how those boots work out for you," he said, shaking hands with a pretty redhead.

The woman started to envelop him in a hug, but drew back when Cassie glared at her. "Sure thing, Guy. I'll do that."

Guy turned to Cassie. "Come on up to my office. I want to check my messages."

"Do you know everyone who shops here?" Cassie asked as they climbed steps to Guy's office.

"A lot of them. Part of the store's success is due to repeat business."

Guy's office was a glass cubicle overlooking the sales floor. It reminded Cassie of a tree house, cluttered with paperwork. His room would have been like this when he was a kid, she decided. It was probably like this now.

Guy thumbed through a stack of message slips on his desk while Cassie watched the activity below. Everywhere she looked people were laughing, talking, trying out gear and spending money. Guy was barely into his thirties and all of this was his. He was powerful and wealthy in a way she'd never known before. And she was a twenty-eight-year-old counter clerk in a coffee shop and massage therapy student. It was too much to take in.

"You ready to get some skis?" Guy touched her shoulder, startling her out of her reverie.

"Sure." She smiled brightly, pushing away her momentary uneasiness. After all, this was Guy. He might be a millionaire genius, but she'd seen him naked.

He escorted her to the ski department and introduced her to a gangly young man with bleached hair and a black goatee. "Jazz here will fix you up," he said. "Jazz, Cassie's going to be competing in the Aspen Creek Downhill. She needs top-of-the-line racing gear."

"No sweat, dude. We've got some really rad new gear that'll have you smokin' down the mountain."

Guy patted Cassie's back. "I'll leave you here to get fitted out while I check on a few things."

"Let's start with boots," Jazz said, pulling out a shoe sizer. "We've got some awesome racing sets."

Cassie sat in a chair in front of the boot display and took off her shoes. "Have you worked for Guy very long?" she asked as Jazz measured her feet.

"Two amazing years." He grinned up at her. "This is, like, my dream job." He held his arms wide. "I get to test all the latest boards and the coolest gear."

"Is Guy a good boss to work for?" *Is he as nice to everyone as he seems?*

"Man, yes! He really digs this stuff, you know? And he understands, you know, if you have to take a day off sometimes because the snow is just too perfect." He plucked a boot from a box and pulled out the liner. "Now stand up in this and let's see how it feels.

"Guy doesn't dis you because your hair's a different color or you're into fashion, you know?" Jazz continued. "He respects everybody as long as they know their job. That looks good. Step out of it a minute." He replaced the liner in the boot and had her try it on again. "How's that?"

"I can't wiggle my toes."

"Sweet! Racing boots are supposed to be tight. Gives you better control, you know? So I'd say this is a perfect fit." He pulled the second boot out of the box. "Put this one on and we'll go over to the skis."

Jazz pulled a pair of hot-pink-and-black skis from a rack on the wall. "We just got these in," he said. "Top of the line, like the man said." He plucked a set of bindings from another rack. "You are gonna be blowin' by the competition."

Jazz was attaching the bindings to the skis when a roar of applause rose up from the middle of the store. "What's that?" Cassie asked.

Jazz looked over her shoulder and grinned. "Just the boss showing off." He nodded toward the commotion. "Go on. It'll take me a few minutes to get these set."

Cassie found a crowd gathered around the climbing rock, their necks craned, watching a familiar figure near the top. Guy clung to a steep face, seemingly hanging on to sheer rock. Even though Cassie could see the safety harness around him, she couldn't hold back a gasp.

"Hey, Cassie!" Guy called down to her. "Come on up. The view's great."

"Oh, no, I don't think—"

But already an employee was pulling her forward, fitting her with a harness and helping her exchange her ski boots for climbing shoes. Guy moved around the side of the rock, to a face obviously designed for beginners, complete with hand and footholds.

Cassie opened her mouth to protest, then she looked up at Guy, at his encouraging smile. Her first thought had been that she couldn't do this, but Guy believed in her. Why shouldn't she try to prove him right?

Cheered on by the crowd, she began to climb. Though the sensation of having nothing but air at her back was disorienting at first, she was soon distracted by the necessity of finding places to put her hands and feet. She discovered muscles she didn't ordinarily use, and an agility she'd never imagined.

Guy met her at the top, pulling her toward him in a hug. "What do you think?" he asked, steadying her in his arms.

"I think I like it." She grinned at him.

He looked around them. "You see things differently from up here," he said.

She turned her back to the scenery, focusing instead on him. She saw *herself* differently when she was with Guy. She wasn't "good old Cassie" with him. Her timid, conventional self had been replaced by a woman daring enough to race down the slopes or scale cliffs. A woman courageous enough to maybe, just maybe, risk her heart.

16

THE DAY BEFORE the Aspen Creek Downhill, Cassie wore the blue embroidered dress she'd bought from Caribe Clothing Company to Dave and Susan's shower. As she slipped it over her head, she remembered the day she'd purchased it, when Guy had stood next to her in the dressing-room stalls, naked. The thought sent heat curling through her, and she silently scolded herself. She had promised herself she was going to think about Guy with her head, not her hormones. How else would she ever figure out what he *really* meant to her?

"Nice dress," he said when she greeted him at the door. He was wearing dark jeans and a fisherman's sweater that set off his wide shoulders and broad chest.

Cassie collected her gift from the hall table. "I got them a wine carafe. I hope that's all right."

"They'll love it. I got them a basketball hoop."

"A basketball hoop?"

"Sure. Every house needs one. And I know Dave likes to play."

When they turned onto the street leading to the house where the shower was being held, Cassie was amazed to see cars parked all up and down the block. "Are all these people here for the shower?" she asked.

"Susan's family has a lot of friends. I imagine there'll be quite a crowd."

No less than thirty couples filled the house in Highlands Ranch, stuffing themselves on sushi and puff pastry tarts and oohing and aahing over a mountain of gifts. Cassie would have bet Guy's basketball hoop was the most unusual gift Dave and Susan received, but she'd have lost. Dave unwrapped a dart board, a power saw and no less than three cordless drills.

She and Guy stood at one side of a massive living room and watched as Susan exclaimed over yet another espresso machine. Dave grinned, not at the coffeemaker, but at his bride-to-be, who really did seem to glow with happiness.

"So what do you think, should they keep the French white china or go with the purple-and-green stoneware?" Guy leaned close to speak softly in her ear.

Cassie glanced at the long table on one side of the room, where place settings of both sets of dishes were piling up. "I like the china," she said, admiring the classic pattern. "It goes with everything."

"I like the stoneware."

Why didn't that surprise her? Could any two people be more different than she and Guy?

"Cassie, darling! I didn't expect to see you here."

Cassie's heart stopped beating as a familiar figure in peach knit rushed toward her. "Mother! What are you doing here?"

"I told you Susan and her parents are friends of the family." Her mother turned to Guy and raised one eyebrow, then looked pointedly at his hand on Cassie's waist. "Aren't you going to introduce me to your friend?"

Cassie moved out of Guy's grasp. "Mother, this is Guy Walters. Guy, this is my mother, May Sanderson."

Guy took May's hand. "Pleased to meet you, Mrs. Sanderson. Now I see where Cassie gets her good looks."

To Cassie's mortification, her mother flushed and giggled. "And how do you know my daughter, Mr. Walters?"

Guy glanced at Cassie, a mischievous look in her eyes. She glared at him, silently threatening him if he dared to tell the truth. "Cassie and I met at a ski resort," he said.

"Walters...Walters." May tapped her finger on her chin. "The name is so familiar. Do I know your family?"

"I don't think so. Maybe you've seen the name in the papers. I own Mountain Outfitters."

"Oooh." May's mouth made a perfect *O*, and Cassie could practically read the dollar signs in her mother's eyes. "Isn't that nice." She leaned toward him, her tone confidential. "And is your relationship with my daughter serious?"

Cassie closed her eyes, wishing the ceiling would cave in on her. Guy chuckled. "I'd like it to be."

"If you'll excuse us a moment, I'd like a word with my daughter." May gripped her arm and pulled Cassie into an alcove outside the doorway. "Did you hear that? He says he'd like your relationship to be serious. What are you going to do about that?"

"Guy is a very nice man, but we don't have anything in common."

"Nonsense. You're both single young people living in the same city. What more do you need?"

She might have known her mother wouldn't understand. "Mom, I like the china and he likes the stoneware." She pointed to the table of dishes. "We have completely different lifestyles."

"Goodness, child, I'm embarrassed to say I raised you." May shook her head. "Don't you know a couple needs *both* kinds of dishes? The china is for special occasions. Use the stoneware every day."

Cassie sighed. "I wasn't really talking about the dishes, Mom."

"I know what you were talking about. Haven't you ever heard that opposites attract?" She gave Cassie a little shove. "Now go back over there and encourage that young man before you've wasted another opportunity."

She returned to Guy's side in time to watch Susan open a box of lingerie. Catcalls and cheers rose from the gathered guests as the bride-to-be held up a leopard-print camisole and matching bikini panties.

"That would look good on you."

Guy's whispered comment sent a shiver down her spine. He slipped his hands around her waist and pulled her back against him, so that she felt his arousal. She closed her eyes and he nuzzled her neck, sending heat through her. "Guy, people are watching," she whispered.

"Mmm." Not changing position, he began easing them backward through the crowd, to the same alcove where Cassie and her mom had talked only moments before. Once there, he turned her toward him, and claimed her mouth with a searing kiss.

She'd missed his kisses, missed losing herself to the dizzying passion that overwhelmed her at his touch. The mistakes of the past, fears about the future and petty annoyances of the present vanished in the sanctuary of his arms. She clung to him, running her hands down his back, reveling in the hard planes of his muscles that seemed to be strong enough for both of them.

Guy kissed her mouth, her throat, the tops of her breasts. A weak voice in the back of her head told her she should stop him, but the daring part of herself she'd kept hidden for so long urged him to take even more liberties. He slid his hand up her skirt, into her panties, until she was light-headed and weak with longing. She wiggled against him and felt for the zipper of his pants. If it was possible to make love in public, standing up, she was determined to do so.

Someone jostled against them, knocking her head back against the wall. Cassie's eyes flew open. "Sorry, I was looking for a phone," a man muttered.

"Get lost, Hamilton," Guy growled.

Cassie gasped. It *was* Bob. Oh, God, could the floor please open up, right now?

Guy eased his hand from beneath Cassie's skirt, but he kept his arms around her. "What are you doing here?" he asked.

Bob crossed his arms over his chest. "Mary Ann is a friend of the bride's." He narrowed his eyes. "What are you doing here, besides necking in the corner?"

Cassie flushed. "We're friends of the groom," Guy said.

Bob looked around. "Pretty nice do, huh? We're thinking of having one of these for our wedding. Why should the bride get all the presents?" He spoke to Guy, but he was looking at Cassie, an unmistakable smirk on his face.

Cassie blinked. His *wedding*?

"Oh, there you are. Did you find a phone?" Mary Ann's three-inch heels clicked toward them. She slipped her arms through Bob's but not before Cassie caught sight of the enormous diamond on the third finger of her left hand.

Bob pulled her close. "I was telling Cassie here about our engagement." He glanced at Cassie again, as if gauging her reaction. "I'm working with Mary Ann at Patterson Publishing, you know." He smiled at his fiancée. "Once we were together every day, we couldn't keep our hands off each other."

Cassie fought an almost uncontrollable urge to laugh. Why had she never seen before how *pathetic* Bob was? She fixed a syrupy sweet smile on her face. "Isn't that wonderful? You two *so* deserve each other."

"Come along, dear. There's someone I want you to meet." Mary Ann fluttered her fingers, the diamond winking at them, and led Bob away.

Guy took Cassie's arm. "Are you okay?"

She sighed and nodded. "Yeah. I'm okay. But I think I'm ready to go home."

"YOU'RE SURE YOU'RE OKAY?" Guy started the car and sat for a moment, waiting for Cassie's answer.

"I don't know whether to laugh at how absurd my life is, or to start breaking things."

Guy bit back a grin. At least she wasn't sobbing. "Like Bob's nose?"

"Or Mary Ann's high heels. Or my mother's copy of *How to Manipulate Your Children for Fun and Profit.*"

"Oh, your mom's not as bad as all that."

"You haven't been around her long enough." She turned toward him. "I get so damned tired of everybody trying to shove me in a little mold. My mom wants me marry the first available man I can trap and produce perfect little grandchildren. Bob expected me to be a convenient doormat and maid, and now he expects me to wither away with jealousy. Nobody ever seems to care about what *I* want to do with my life."

"Do you lump me in with all those other people, too?"

She looked away. "I don't know. Maybe."

He put the car into gear. "Instead of going home, I've got a better idea."

They headed out of Highlands Ranch, toward Golden. The dark hulk of the mountains rose on their left, moonlight reflected on the snowy peaks. Suburbs gave way to open fields washed in silver light. Stars shone overhead like pinholes in black paper.

He waited for Cassie to ask where they were headed, but she was silent, staring out the window. He wondered if she was even seeing the scenery, or if she was lost in her own thoughts.

After half an hour of driving, he slowed and signaled a turn into Heritage Amusement Park. Cassie sat up. "What are you doing?" she asked. "The park's not open this time of year."

"The Ferris wheel and the carousel are open." They drove under the wrought-iron archway, past the silent hulk of the Scorpion and the shrouded teacup ride, past shuttered souvenir booths and refreshment stands, to the giant Ferris wheel.

It rose against the night sky, jeweled with lights. As they got out of the car, tinny music from the nearby merry-go-round greeted them, like a tune played on a child's piano.

Guy checked his watch. "Come on. It's almost closing time."

"Guy, we're not going to ride that thing!" she called, even as she ran after him.

A grizzled man in a cracked bomber jacket and trapper's cap stepped out of the attendant's booth as they approached. "Sorry, folks, time to shut her down."

"Only a few minutes more." Guy pulled out his wallet and stuffed a twenty in the man's hand. "One ride to the top."

The man studied them a moment, then stuffed the bill in his pocket and turned back to the booth, muttering about love-struck kids and their crazy ideas.

"Guy, I'm serious. I'm not getting on that thing." She pulled her coat more closely around her. "It's freezing out here."

"I'll keep you warm." He put his arm around her shoulders and pulled her close, walking her over to the bottom basket.

CASSIE TOLD HERSELF she ought to resist, but already she was caught up in the excitement, wondering what Guy would do next. He settled in beside her and pulled her close as the old man shut the door behind them. "See, I won't let you be cold."

"You're nuts." Even as she said it, she snuggled closer, inhaling the leather-and-spice scent of his cologne, reveling in the feel of his strong arms around her.

Gears clanked, their carriage swayed and jerked, and then the giant wheel began to turn. They rose up, up, the ground falling away below them. They swung out into blackness and Cassie stifled a scream and squeezed shut her eyes. Guy took her hands in his and held them. "Open your eyes," he whispered.

She gasped at the panorama before her. The lights of Denver twinkled like a treasure trove of jewels against the velvet-dark backdrop of the mountains. Who could be cold with such splendor before them?

Their car reached the apex of the wheel and stopped moving. They hung suspended, letting the sights and sounds of the moment wash over them. The car squeaked as it rocked gently back and forth, and far below she heard the rumble of a truck on the highway. But even these sounds were swallowed up in the immense silence.

After a long while, she turned to look at Guy. "Why did you bring me up here?"

"First answer a question for me."

"Maybe." She wasn't ready to bare her soul for him—yet.

"When you saw Bob with Mary Ann this evening, were you hurt?"

She shook her head. "No."

"Then why did you act upset? And want to leave?" He touched her face, his fingers warm in spite of the chill in the air.

A tightness in her throat made it hard to say anything. She looked out at the view, trying to control her chaotic emotions. "I was angry at myself—that I'd let him manipulate me for so long," she said after a moment. "It's hard for me to admit I screwed up that way."

"We're always harder on ourselves than we are on other people." He slid his hand around to caress her neck, a motion both soothing and seductive. "I brought you up here to give you a little perspective. To make you realize the possibilities. No matter what you think, no matter what your mother or Bob or anyone else has told you, you have that passion in you to do anything you want. That's not ordinary, Cassie. It's a rare gift."

She turned to him once more, not drawing away when he leaned in to kiss her, but welcoming his touch. She'd been so afraid to want this, afraid the things she'd felt since that night in Aspen Creek were the stuff of fantasy, never meant to be real.

But Guy's lips on her now were real, his arms encircling her, pulling her close, were strong and warm and oh, so real. He caressed her neck, fingers tracing the curve of her jaw, trailing down her throat and along her collarbone, then dropping to her breasts, stroking her achingly erect nipples through the soft cotton of her dress.

She moaned, arching toward him, and he deepened the kiss, his tongue delving, teasing, coaxing. His hand dropped lower, to her belly, then slid beneath her skirt. His calloused fingers grazed the smooth skin of her stomach. He moved up, cradling her breast in his palm, his thumb flicking across the sensitive tip.

She tensed, struggling to hold back a moan, and shifted against him, trying to get closer still. Was it possible to make love in a Ferris wheel basket ten stories above the ground?

A jolt threw them together, and the basket began its descent. Guy raised his head and smiled down on her. "Still cold?"

She shook her head. She didn't think she'd ever be cold again.

On the ground again, Guy helped her from the basket and thanked the attendant, who leered at them. Arm in arm, they walked across the parking lot, not speaking.

Neither said much on the drive back to her apartment. The moment seemed to Cassie too precious to spoil with words.

He walked her to her door and waited while she opened it, but to her surprise, declined to come in. "I'd like to, but I think I'd better not." He took a step back, hands shoved in the pockets of his jacket. "I want you to know this isn't just about sex for me, Cassie. I want more from you and I'm willing to wait until you're ready to give it." He leaned forward and kissed her cheek, then turned and left, leaving her more than a little frustrated and confused.

Beneath those surface feelings, though, rose something deeper. Guy had talked of passion, and then shown her how strong such feelings could be. Strong enough to defeat doubt and fear. Strong enough to make her believe a fantasy could become real.

17

"YOU CAN DO THIS. You can do this. You can do this." Cassie recited this mantra as she rushed about her apartment the morning of the race. Where was her water bottle? What had she done with her gloves? What had she been thinking to ever want to do this in the first place?

By the time the doorbell rang, she had chewed off all her fingernails and was bemoaning the waste of a manicure. She jerked open the door, prepared to wail out her fears to Guy; instead, Jill was standing there.

"What are you doing here?" Cassie asked.

"I came to take you to Aspen Creek."

"Where's Guy?" She leaned out the door and looked down the hall past Jill.

"He's gone on ahead. Said he had some things to take care of." Jill strolled into the apartment. "So how do you feel?"

Cassie closed the door and leaned against it. "Like I'm going to be sick."

"You do look a little peaked. Here." Jill opened her purse and took out a compact. She opened it and leaned forward, makeup brush in hand. "I'll just add a little color—"

Cassie darted away. "Jill, this is a ski race, not a beauty contest."

Jill replaced the brush in the compact. "Yeah, but don't forget who's waiting at the end of the course."

Cassie sagged onto the couch. "He's part of the problem."

Jill sat beside her. "You mean to tell me after all these mornings jogging together, Saturdays skiing together and evenings eating together you two still haven't gotten it together?"

"He took me to ride on a Ferris wheel last night."

Jill's eyebrows shot up. "For real? Or is that some new sexual position I haven't heard about?"

Cassie nodded. "For real. We went to Heritage Park and he paid an old guy twenty dollars to let us ride on the Ferris wheel. In the dark."

Jill grinned. "That's a new one. So what happened when he got you up there?"

"He kissed me."

"The man's got style, I have to say that."

Style and sex appeal out the ears and the ability to leave her completely confused.

"So what's wrong?" Jill asked. Her expression changed to one of alarm. "You didn't turn him down, did you? You aren't still playing the ice maiden?"

"There was nothing to turn down. He took me home and left me on the doorstep."

"That's it? Did he say anything?"

"He said he wanted me to know this was about more than sex with him." She chewed her lower lip. "What do you think it means?"

"I think it means he's really serious. He's in love

with you." She leaned toward Cassie. "The question is, are you in love with him?"

"I think so," she whispered. She could hardly talk around the knot in her chest. Saying the words made her feel like she'd just gone off a ski jump, terrified and exhilarated all at the same time.

"Then all you have to do is tell him." Jill patted her shoulder and stood. "Come on, we've got to go. Guy's waiting."

GUY HAD BEEN at Aspen Creek since seven-thirty that morning, signing Cassie in, getting her gear laid out and studying the course. By almost nine, he'd had three cups of coffee, eaten four antacid tablets and worn a trench in the snow from pacing back and forth.

"Will you settle down?" Amy snapped.

He shaded his eyes with his hand and squinted toward the top of the slope where the race course had been laid out. "I don't know about this sun. Do you think it's getting icy up top?"

"The course looks fine. Now settle down. You're making *me* nervous."

He glanced at her. "Did you get the things I asked you?"

"Before I answer that, tell me one thing."

"I don't have time for twenty questions right now, sis."

"Just one question."

He tore his gaze away from the course and focused on his sister. "All right. What's the question?"

"Do you love Cassie?"

"Yes." No hesitation. Being with Cassie made him

feel complete. No more missing pieces or wondering about the future. As long as the future included Cassie, it would be all right.

"And does she love you?"

"That's two questions."

She reached out and pinched his arm. "Answer me."

He looked away, toward the parking lot, where Cassie and Jill should be arriving at any minute. "I think she does. She hasn't admitted it yet, but she will."

Amy followed his gaze to the course. "Did I ever tell you she tried to talk me out of making that last run the day I was injured?"

He stared at his sister. Her gaze was fixed on the top of the race course, but he had a feeling she wasn't seeing it the way it looked today. "No, you never told me that."

"The sun had come out and iced over the churned up snow. Cassie made the run right before me and she called back up to the gate to say it was too dangerous." Her gaze flickered to him, old pain showing clearly. "I argued with her. Called her a coward."

He put his arm around Amy's shoulders and pulled her close. "You didn't know what would happen."

She looked at the ground. "When I saw her after the surgery, all I could think of was how stupid I'd been. Stupid not to listen to her. Stupid to confuse judgment with fear."

"Everybody makes mistakes. Sometimes they cost us more than we want to pay."

She squeezed his waist, then stepped back. "I'll help you out. But if she lets you down, I swear, I'll never speak to her again."

"She won't let me down." Whether love or foolishness made him so certain, he guessed he'd find out. He returned to scanning the crowd, and spotted Cassie and Jill moving toward them. Cassie was wearing her pink jacket, the one she'd worn the night she'd come to his door here at Aspen Creek. His pulse quickened. Would it always be this way, losing track of everything else whenever she walked into view?

"Sorry we're late," Jill panted. "I made a wrong turn coming in and had to circle around to find the participants' parking."

Guy looked at Cassie. "How are you feeling?"

She nodded. "Okay. A little nervous."

"You're going to do fine." He picked up a clipboard. "You're number eighteen. You're skiing right after Tammy Simmons."

Cassie rolled her eyes. "What a tough act to follow."

He rubbed her shoulders. "You'll do fine."

"Hey, Cassie! Guy!"

He looked up and instantly felt the need for more antacid tablets. Make that the whole bottle. Bob and Mary Ann were making their way toward them through the crowd.

"What are you doing here?" Cassie asked. "You don't even like skiing."

He put his arm around Mary Ann. "Mary Ann's father is one of the sponsors so we got free tickets."

"Bob would watch snake wrestling if the tickets were free," Jill mumbled.

"Bob tells me you're racing today," Mary Ann said to Cassie.

"I hear Tammy Simmons is favored to win," Bob said.

Guy fought the urge to plant the man in the nearest snowbank. He glanced at Cassie to see how she was taking this. Her face was red, and she glared at Bob.

"See you later." Bob waved and led Mary Ann away.

Guy put his hand on Cassie's shoulder. "Are you ready?"

"Just a minute." She bent and scooped up a handful of the slushy snow and mud where he'd been pacing and packed it into a tight ball. She pulled back her arm and sent the snowball sailing in a perfect arc, to explode against the back of Bob's head with a resounding *splat!*

Bob yelped and frantically fished snow from his collar. Cassie grinned and brushed the snow from her hands. "Now I'm ready."

The P.A. buzzed. "Racers, please take your places."

Guy leaned forward to kiss Cassie's cheek. "Remember passion," he whispered.

REMEMBER PASSION. The word hadn't meant much to her before she met Guy. With him, she'd experienced a physical passion she'd never known before. He'd shown her other passions, too—a passion for skiing she'd all but forgotten, and an excitement and enthusiasm for life she'd thought had passed her by.

She watched him as he paced back and forth in the coaches' area. He studied the clipboard in his hand and made notes about the course, kept track of other players' times, and scribbled incomprehensible doodles. He was so intense, so focused on this event, on her.

One of the junior racers, a girl about twelve, starry-eyed and nervous, came up to him with a question about her skis. As a sponsor of the event, Mountain Outfitters had provided gear for several racers in addition to Cassie.

He knelt and helped the girl adjust her bindings. Even from this distance, Cassie could sense the girl's nervousness leave. Guy was like that. He was good at putting people at ease. At helping them.

The call came for the first of two runs to begin and she hurried to take her place. After training for two weeks, the day was flying by too quickly. She'd wanted to savor the moment, to commit to memory everything about her first big race, but found herself instead hurtling through the day almost as quickly as she hurtled down the runs.

At the end of the first run, she was in sixth place. Guy came up to her after the run to offer her tips and to reassure her she was doing great. Not that she needed him to tell her that—she could feel it in every cell. And she could hear it in the murmurs of those around her. Who was this nobody who had worked her way to sixth place in the race?

She was getting ready to take her place in line for the last run when Amy came running up to her. "I wanted to say good luck. And to give you this." She shoved something into Cassie's hand.

Cassie unfolded her fingers and stared at the tiny green-haired troll doll in her palm. "It's your good-luck charm," she said softly.

"Yeah." Amy squeezed her arm. "I'm sorry I've

been such a jerk. I thought I was mad at you for giving up something I loved so much, but I think I was really mad at myself for getting hurt in the first place."

Cassie tucked the troll doll into her jumpsuit. It made a hard lump close to her heart. "Thanks," she said, tears stinging her eyes. "I've really missed you."

"I've missed you, too." Amy stepped back and waved her on. "You'd better get in line. And remember what our coach at CU always said: 'Anybody can win a race. You just have to really want it.'"

Cassie stared after Amy, thinking about what she'd said. What did *she* really want?

She wanted to be herself—not the nice, quiet, good old Cassie Bob had made her into, or the wild woman she'd been that night with Guy. Just...Cassie, nice sometimes and wild sometimes.

She wanted to do something useful in life. Massage therapy fit the bill there, though there were people who would probably say coffee was every bit as important to them.

She wanted Guy. She had wanted him from the first time he'd walked into the coffee shop—maybe even before. She hadn't stopped wanting him since their magical night together here at Aspen Creek. All this time she'd been focusing on the ways they were different, blind to all the things they shared. Like ski racers, they had different styles. Cassie was calmer, more traditional. Guy was more flamboyant, ready to try new things. But they were both intense. Passionate. Together, maybe they could find the perfect balance.

"Number eighteen. In the gate."

Heart pounding, she took her place at the starting gate, the steep slope stretched out before her. Sun glinted on the tracks other skiers had made and the flags on the gates popped in the wind. The starting buzzer sounded and she flew out of the gate, knees bent, poles tucked. She hit the first turn and shifted her weight to take it on one ski. Icy wind stung her cheeks and the *snkkk, snkkk,* of her ski edges cutting into the snow filled her ears. Two more turns and she tucked tighter for the race home. She was flying, soaring over the snow like a bird. Her goal was the finish line, and Guy. She had to tell him what she'd learned up here on the slopes, what she'd discovered about her feelings for him and their chance for a future together. The roar of the crowd matched the pounding of her heart as she crested the last hill and plunged toward the finish line.

Speed blurred her vision as she crossed the finish line. She threw herself into a curve, sending up a spray of snow. Amy and Jill rushed forward to embrace her. "Look at your time! Look at your time!" Amy pointed toward the digital display above them—1:12.23.

She blinked, not sure she'd read it right. "Where does that put me in the standings?" she asked.

"You're in second place!" Jill pounded her on the back.

"Where's Guy?" She had to tell Guy.

Amy's grin held a hint of mischief. "Oh, Guy couldn't be here. He's busy."

"Busy?" Her spirits plummeted. "He's my coach. He's supposed to be here."

"Hush. They're announcing the winners." Jill grabbed her hand and squeezed it.

"In third place, Martinique Collier."

Cassie squeezed her eyes shut, not daring to breathe.

"Second place goes to Cassie Carmichael."

The rest of the announcer's words were drowned out by Amy and Jill's squeals, and her own triumphant shout. Five minutes later, she joined Martinique and Tammy at the winner's podium and accepted her medal. From the awards stand, she scanned the crowd, looking for Guy. Where the heck was he?

As she was leaving the awards stand, a teenage boy approached, carrying a sheaf of flowers. "Cassie Carmichael?" he asked.

"Yes."

"These are for you." He handed her the bouquet of daisies and turned to leave.

"Wait! Who are they from?"

"There's a card."

She searched through the paper, but the only card she found was for Aspen Creek Condominiums. *Suite 406* was scrawled across it. And after that: *But only if you're sure.*

She stared at the card, then began to laugh. "Oh, Guy, I'm sure," she whispered. "I've never been more sure of anything in my life."

Declining invitations to head to a local brewpub to party with the other winners, she slipped away from the crowd and headed for the condos and number 406.

Guy greeted her at the door, dressed in a green velour bathrobe and holding two glasses of champagne. "Amy phoned me the good news." He handed her one of the glasses and ushered her into the room. "Congratulations."

"It was only second place," she said, unable to sound entirely modest. She sipped the champagne, its bubbles scarcely able to compete with the anticipation bubbling inside her.

"I'd say second place in your first race, behind Tammy Simmons, is pretty damned good."

"So now we celebrate?" She set her glass on the mantle and reached for the zipper on her ski suit.

"Hold it." He took her hand, his thumb stroking her knuckles. "I seem to recall last time we were here, you seduced me."

Heat curled through her. "I...I seem to recall that, too."

His lips curved in a lazy, seductive smile. "Now it's my turn."

She tilted her head up for his kiss, but he merely smiled and began to unzip her ski suit. Every nerve tingled with an awareness of him. The brush of his hand across her stomach as he lowered the zipper made her quiver. When he peeled the suit and her sports bra back from her shoulder and kissed the skin where her neck and shoulder met, she trembled.

"Oh, Guy, hurry," she urged. She had waited so long. Why had she waited?

"No rush," he murmured, his mouth leaving a trail of heat along her collarbone. "We've got plenty of time."

She moaned as his tongue traced a circle around her nipple, drawing closer and closer, but never quite touching, the sensitive tip. He moved to the other breast, repeating the teasing attention. She rested her head against his shoulder and moaned.

He knelt before her and helped her take off her boots, then slid the suit down her body. She stepped out of it and stood before him in her underwear. Still kneeling, he kissed the inside of her thigh, wet, hot kisses that moved closer...closer to the center of her desire. She closed her eyes and swayed. "Guy, if you keep that up, I don't think I can stand up."

He rose, his body brushing up against hers, and gathered her into his arms. "I can fix that." He scooped her up and carried her into the bedroom, tugging away her panties as he deposited her on the bed.

"No fair my being naked when you're not," she said.

He grinned and loosened the tie of the robe. "How's this?" He threw back his shoulders and let the robe fall away. She swallowed hard.

Lamplight burnished his skin to bronze, highlighting every muscle, shadowing every hollow. She wanted to touch him, to run her hands across his broad chest, down his arms to his narrow waist, to reassure herself he was real.

Her gaze dropped to below his waist, to his arousal, clear evidence of his desire for her. It strained toward her, promising ecstasy. "Guy, hurry."

He stretched out on the bed beside her, almost, but not quite touching. "No hurry," he said again, and smoothed his hand along her body from shoulder to hip.

Everywhere he touched her was hot, melting. She rolled toward him, bringing her body against his. "Kiss me," she demanded.

He did so, not only with his lips, but with his whole body caressing her, loving her. While his lips and tongue explored the contours of her mouth, his hands smoothed and kneaded her back, her buttocks, her thighs. He pulled her firm against him, close, but not yet close enough.

Then he pulled away, ignoring her cries and reaching hands as he lowered his head to her breasts once more. He licked and suckled, sending wave after wave of sensation through her, bringing her ever closer to the edge, but never quite there.

When he drew away once more, she was weak and trembling with need. Was she imagining things, or did his hands tremble as he reached for a condom?

Guy had waited as long as he dared. He closed his eyes and breathed deeply, struggling for control. He wanted this night to be special. One neither of them would ever forget.

When he thought he could go on, he quickly sheathed himself and knelt between Cassie's legs. She looked up at him, eyes heavy-lidded with desire, mouth swollen from his kisses. "I love you, Cassie," he said, the first time he had ever expressed the feeling out loud. He slid into her, slowly, deeply, wanting her to feel how much he meant the words.

"Oh, Guy, I love y—" His first thrust turned her words to a moan, which he met with a cry of his own.

With his thumb, he caressed the sensitive nub at her center, smiling as she cried out and arched against him. His thrusts grew more urgent, and his vision blurred as he surrendered to the rising tide of passion.

They moved in concert, clinging to one another, unbearable tension building...building...

"Guy!" Cassie sobbed his name as she arched against him, her face flushed with passion.

He quickly followed, every nerve jolted by the force of his release. "Cassie!"

When he found the strength to open his eyes once more, he found her staring at him, cheeks wet with tears. Alarmed, he pulled her closer. "What's wrong? Did I hurt you?"

She shook her head. "No. I...to think I was so afraid...for nothing."

He cradled her head on his shoulder, rocking her like a child. "I love you," he said, and again. "I love you."

"I love you, too, Guy." She stroked his chest, her fingers featherlight against his skin. "Not Guy Walters, the fantasy man, but the real Guy."

He smiled. "What's the difference between the real Guy and the fantasy man?"

She raised her head and looked into his eyes. "The real Guy gave me passion. For love, and for life."

"I didn't give it to you. You already had it." He pulled the covers up over them and caressed her shoulder. "So what's next? I hear there's a ski race next month at Copper Mountain."

"I'm ready if you are, coach."

"I'm ready." He stroked her cheek with one finger. "And I've been thinking—we already have a coffee shop at Mountain Outfitters, maybe it's time we added a massage therapist."

She stared at him. "Are you serious?"

"Why not. People could come in for a massage or for

therapy for a sports injury. We might start a real trend. That is, if I can find the right therapist for the job."

"I might know of someone. But she doesn't graduate until May."

"I can wait."

She took a deep breath, mustering courage. "I've been thinking about other things I want to do with my life, too."

He raised one eyebrow. "Such as?"

She snuggled closer. "What would you think of a mountaintop wedding?"

"As long as I get to be the groom this time, I'm all for it."

"But no sky divers," she said. "I'm still an ordinary girl at heart."

"You were never ordinary, Cassie. Not to me." He kissed her. The woman who would be his wife. The woman who had captured his heart.

A visit to Cooper's Corner offers the chance for a new beginning...

C O O P E R ' S   C O R N E R

Coming in December 2002
DANCING IN THE DARK
by Sandra Marton

Check-in: When Wendy Monroe left Cooper's Corner, she was an Olympic hopeful in skiing...and madly in love with Seth Castleman. But an accident on the slopes shattered her dreams, and rather than tell Seth the painful secret behind her injuries, Wendy leaves him.

Checkout: A renowned surgeon staying at Twin Oaks can mend Wendy's leg. But only facing Seth again—and the truth—can mend her broken heart.

HARLEQUIN®
Makes any time special ®

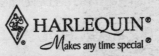

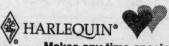

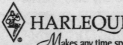